Flying High!

Discover the poetry in British birds

Anneliese Emmans Dean

Brambleby Books Ltd.

Flying High! Discover the poetry in British birds
Text © Anneliese Emmans Dean 2017
Photographs © individual photographers as specified in the Acknowledgements

*Anneliese Emmans Dean has asserted her right
under the Copyright, Designs and Patents Act, 1988,
to be identified as the Author of this work.*

All rights reserved.
No part of this book may be reproduced in any form
by photocopying or by any electronic or mechanical means,
including information, storage or retrieval systems,
without permission in writing from both the copyright
owner and the publisher of this book.

ISBN 9781908241504

First published in 2017 by
Brambleby Books Ltd, UK
www.bramblebybooks.co.uk

Cover design and book layout by Tanya Warren
Front cover photo (Blue Tit) © Lee Walker
Photo of Anneliese Emmans Dean on page 8 by AR Marketing

Printed and bound on FSC paper by GraphyCems, Spain

Acknowledgements

Thank you to all the grown-ups
who bought me bird books when I was young.

And to my primary-school teacher Mr Dolman
and my secondary-school teacher Mrs Green
for bringing me to poetry, and poetry to me.

Thank you, too, to all the talented photographers listed below,
whose fabulous photos appear in this book.

Chris Bainbridge: Chaffinch 69, 76–77
Jayne Booton, Shropshire: Goldfinches 112–113; Herring Gull 121
Lindsey Bowes (flickr.com/photos/elbowes): Great Crested Grebes 41, 63, 64
Mark Coates (flickr.com/photos/gm_coates): Blue Tit 88i, 121; Dunnock 121; Greylag Goose 121; Herring Gull 41; Kestrel 94; Mallard 121; Mute Swan 12–13, 130–131; Oystercatcher 36i; Pheasant 15, 22i; Pied Wagtail 40, 58–59; Robin 121; Tree Sparrow 88i
Edd Cottell (eddcottell.co.uk): Hen Harrier 41, 46i; Starling murmuration 98i
Gary Faulkner: Blackbird 41, 66–67; Bullfinch 106i; Chiffchaff 15, 18–19; Dipper 69, 90–91; House Martin 60i; Linnet 69, 80–81; Little Owl 69, 82–83; Oystercatcher chick 15, 36i; Swallow 24i; Waxwing 95, 118–119; Wren 40, 42–43
Clare Forster: Coot 100i
Steve R Jellett (flickr.com/photos/hc1): House Sparrow 78–79
Caroline Jones: Rookery 32i
Ian Kirk: Herring Gull 44–45; Long-tailed Tits 68, 70–71; Magpie 15, 30–31
Derek Lees: Fieldfare 69, 92–93

Raymond Leinster: Buzzard 41, 56–57
Roy Lowry (flickr.com/photos/99817330@N02): Coot 95, 100–101; Dunnock 95, 110–111; Great Tit 52i; Grey Heron 69, 72–73; Greylag Geese 68, 86–87; Kestrel 104–105; Mallard 62–63
Tom McKinney: Pink-footed Geese 86i
James McNie (ipernity.com/home/coldwaterjohn): Oystercatcher egg 36–37
Linda Martin Photography (flickr.com/photos/lindamartinphotos): Blackbird 14, 16–17
Mark Ollett (markollett.com): Pheasants 22–23
Lewis Outing: Mallards 65
Andrew Page (andrewjohnpage.com): Great Tit 41, 52–53
Chris Paul: Mistle Thrush 15, 34–35
Graham Price: Greenfinch 20i
Bill Smith (Smithbill327flickr): Starlings 95, 98–99
Richard Steel (wildlifephotographic.blogspot.co.uk): Goldfinch 94; Puffin 134–135; Song Thrush 69, 88–89
Cheryl Tate (flickr.com/photos/70382111@N02): Great Tits 52i

Lee Walker: Blue Tit (front cover)
Antony Ward (flickr.com/photos/antonyward): Bullfinch 95, 106–107; Cuckoo 15, 28–29; House Martin 41, 60–61; Siskin 95, 114–115
Andy Webster: Rook 14, 32–33
Mandy West (walkingwithwildlife.webs.com): Hen Harrier 46–47; Swift 41, 54–55
Terry Weston: Kingfisher 11, 69, 84i; Swallow 121
George Wilkinson (flickr.com/photos/97496243@N06): Ring-necked Parakeet 95, 108–109
Phil Winter (flickr.com/photos/philwinter): Blackbirds 40, 50–51; Chiffchaff 121; Great Spotted Woodpecker 15, 26–27; Green Woodpecker 95, 102–103; Greenfinch 15, 20–21; Kingfisher 84–85; Mistle Thrushes 15, 38–39; Robin 94, 96–97; Swallow 14, 24–25; Tawny Owls 95, 116–117; Wren 121

i = insert photo
Any photos not listed here were taken by me.

Dedication

To budding birders
Finn
Paddy
and Conor

In memory of
Alfred N. Colley
1917 – 2015
who inspired in his pupils
a love of nature

Contents

About the Author 8
Foreword 9
Bill Board 10
Let's Fly High! 12

Spring 14
Blackbird – The Takeover 16
Chiffchaff – Who's Calling? 18
Greenfinch – Colour Coded 20
Pheasant – On Guard! 22
Swallow – Intercontinental 24
Great Spotted Woodpecker –
  Zero-Concussion Percussion 26
Cuckoo – Hark the Herald 28
Magpie – Daylight Robbery 30
Rook – Conviviality 32
Mistle Thrush –
  Incubation, Incubation, Incubation 34
Oystercatcher – The Great Escape 36
Mistle Thrush –
  Parental Responsibility 38

Summer 40
Wren – The Voice 42
Herring Gull – Air Strikes 44
Hen Harrier – Endangered 46
Blue Tit – Homesick 48
Blackbird – Pester Power 50
Great Tit – Me Time 52
Swift – Fast 54
Buzzard – High Rise 56
Pied Wagtail – The Fidget 58
House Martin – FlapChat 60
Great Crested Grebe
& Mallard – Different Strokes 62
Blackbird – Taking the Heat 66

Autumn   68

- Long-tailed Tit – Tell-Tales   70
- Grey Heron – Cool, Calm, Collected   72
- Feral Pigeon – Putting the Moves On   74
- Chaffinch – Bath Time!   76
- House Sparrow – Spick and Span   78
- Linnet – What's in a Name?   80
- Little Owl – Night and Day   82
- Kingfisher – Streaker   84
- Greylag Goose – Formation Flying   86
- Song Thrush – Real Meal Deal   88
- Dipper – Aquanaut   90
- Fieldfare – Far Afield   92

Winter   94

- Robin – Ho Ho Ho!   96
- Starling – Startling   98
- Coot – The Bald Truth   100
- Green Woodpecker – Lawn Maintenance   102
- Kestrel – Windhover   104
- Bullfinch – Round   106
- Ring-necked Parakeet – Out of Place   108
- Dunnock – Look and Learn   110
- Goldfinch – Collective Invective   112
- Siskin – The Jizz   114
- Tawny Owl – Stereo   116
- Waxwing – Winter Wonder   118

Up, Up & Away!   120

- Bird Words   122
- Index   130
- Over to You …   132
- Find Out More …   134
- The End   135

About the Author

Anneliese Emmans Dean is an award-winning poet and performer, and a life-long lover of birds. She's passionate about inspiring learning through laughter, rhythm and rhyme.

Anneliese delights audiences in schools, festivals and beyond with her 'edu-taining' poetry shows, in which she brings her *Flying High!* and *Buzzing!* books to life.

Anneliese's first book, *Buzzing! Discover the poetry in garden minibeasts*, was shortlisted for the Royal Society Young People's Book Prize and won the NS Teachers' Book Award for Poetry. It's a National Insect Week recommended book.

Flying High! does for birds what *Buzzing!* did for minibeasts – it combines poetry, science and giggles. It's the bird book Anneliese wishes she'd had when she was growing up.

Anneliese has been commissioned to write and perform poems by a wide range of people and organisations, including the Bumblebee Conservation Trust, the Radio 2 Arts Show, Radio 4's Woman's Hour and the BBC World Service.

Anneliese studied at Cambridge University and now lives back in York, where she first started birdwatching when she was little, and where she's a patron of her local nature reserve.

Find out more at Anneliese's website: www.theBigBuzz.biz

Foreword

If you're a grown-up who cares about wildlife, one of the most important things you can do is encourage young people to share your enjoyment and enthusiasm. I conspicuously failed! I tried, I really tried, but my own (grown-up) children and my five grandchildren, whilst not hostile to nature, don't 'get it'. To be honest they think Grandad is, well, a bit daft. But I can't help feeling that if only this marvellous little book had been available years ago, things might just have turned out differently.

Flying High! brings together poetry, science and great pictures in an engaging mix. I'm a scientist, and Anneliese's descriptions of bird biology (their life-cycles, behaviour, ecology and so on) are spot on. But what makes the book different are the poems. I loved them. They made me chuckle, even laugh out loud, with pleasure. They capture the essence of each bird quite brilliantly. I wish I could have read them to my own children when they were young. But children of all ages will enjoy them today, and if you do, you will never look at a Long-tailed Tit, a Herring Gull or a Dipper in quite the same way again.

Professor Sir John Lawton CBE FRS
Vice-President, Royal Society for the Protection of Birds (RSPB)
Former Vice-President, British Trust for Ornithology (BTO)
President, Yorkshire Wildlife Trust

Bill Board

If you've never heard
Of a tricky bird word
Look it up here
And I'll make it clear!

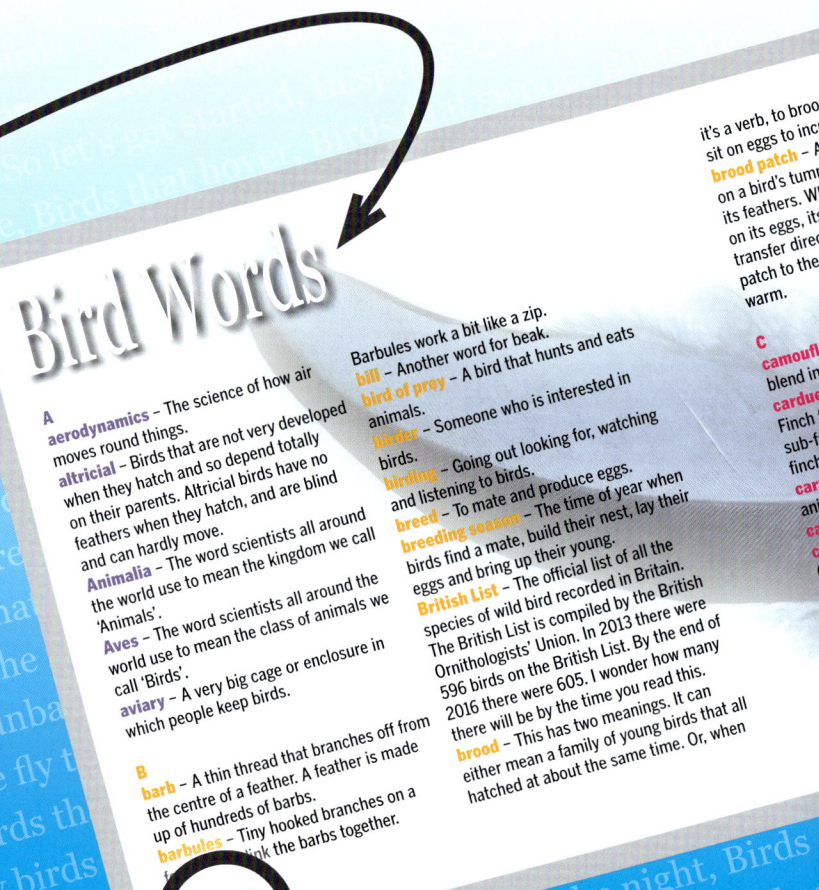

Bird Words

A
aerodynamics – The science of how air moves round things.
altricial – Birds that are not very developed when they hatch and so depend totally on their parents. Altricial birds have no feathers when they hatch, and are blind and can hardly move.
Animalia – The word scientists all around the world use to mean the kingdom we call 'Animals'.
Aves – The word scientists all around the world use to mean the class of animals we call 'Birds'.
aviary – A very big cage or enclosure in which people keep birds.

B
barb – A thin thread that branches off from the centre of a feather. A feather is made up of hundreds of barbs.
barbules – Tiny hooked branches on a [feather that] link the barbs together. Barbules work a bit like a zip.
bill – Another word for beak.
bird of prey – A bird that hunts and eats animals.
birder – Someone who is interested in birds.
birding – Going out looking for, watching and listening to birds.
breed – To mate and produce eggs.
breeding season – The time of year when birds find a mate, build their nest, lay their eggs and bring up their young.
British List – The official list of all the species of wild bird recorded in Britain. The British List is compiled by the British Ornithologists' Union. In 2013 there were 596 birds on the British List. By the end of 2016 there were 605. I wonder how many there will be by the time you read this.
brood – This has two meanings. It can either mean a family of young birds that all hatched at about the same time. Or, when it's a verb, to brood [means to] sit on eggs to incu[bate them].
brood patch – A [bare patch] on a bird's tumm[y where] its feathers [are missing. When a bird sits] on its eggs, its [warmth can] transfer direct[ly from the brood] patch to the e[ggs to keep them] warm.

C
camoufla[ge] – [to] blend in [with surroundings]
carduel[inae] – Finch fa[mily] sub-fa[mily of] finche[s]
carri[on] – anim[al remains]
cav[ity]
ch[ick]

class – Scientists divide up living things into different categories, starting with five kingdoms. Kingdoms are divided up into phyla. Phyla are divided up into smaller groups called classes. One of these is a class called 'Birds' (Aves).

clutch – The number of eggs that a bird lays (and then incubates) at one time.

collective noun – The word we use to describe a group of a particular animal. For example, a 'charm' of Goldfinches, a 'murder' of crows, a 'wisdom' of owls.

coo – The sound pigeons make.

courtship – Special behaviour to attract a mate.

D

dabble – To move the bill around in shallow water, filtering out tiny plants and animals to eat. Many species of duck do this.

dawn chorus – Lots of different birds singing early in the morning, starting at around dawn. The dawn chorus happens from about March to July. Birds that sing in it include Robins, Blackbirds, Wrens, finches, sparrows and thrushes.

123

Let's Fly High!

Come fly through the seasons
Bird by bird
Yes, fly through the seasons
Oh my word

You'll meet birds that sing
Birds that caw
Birds that delight
Birds that bore

Birds that hover
Birds that swoop
Birds that skim
And loop the loop

Birds that fish
Birds pecking seeds
Birds that hunt
For four-legged feeds

Birds of the night
Birds of the day
Birds that are visitors
Birds that stay

You'll learn how birds nest
How birds hatch
What birds do
To defend their patch

How birds wash
How birds preen
How some sunbathe
To help keep clean

There's incubation
And a murmuration
A V-formation
And, of course, migration

There are facts and figures
Rhythm and rhyme
So let's get started
In spring-time!

Spring

Blackbird	16
Chiffchaff	18
Greenfinch	20
Pheasant	22
Swallow	24
Great Spotted Woodpecker	26
Cuckoo	28
Magpie	30
Rook	32
Mistle Thrush	34
Oystercatcher	36
Mistle Thrush	38

Blackbird

The Takeover

I'm building my nest in your garden
I need grasses, dead leaves and some moss
You can't cut your hedge
Until my offspring fledge
From now on it's me here who's boss.

I'm building my nest in your garden
I've got my own special technique
I clear out the clutter
That's clogging your gutter
Then dredge out the mud with my beak.

I'm building my nest in your garden
That there Song Thrush will have to BACK OFF!
To bring up my brood
I'll need plenty of food
I'm not sharing my space with that toff.

I've built my nest in your garden
Well hidden and out of harm's way
It's comfy and sturdy
Very Blackbirdy
So now, I'm ready to lay.

BIRD BOX

Common name	Blackbird
Scientific name	*Turdus merula*
Family	Chats & Thrushes | Turdidae
Order	Passerines | Passeriformes
Class	Birds | Aves
Phylum	Vertebrates | Chordata
Kingdom	Animals | Animalia
Length	25–28cm

EGGHEAD

- In spring, most British birds start to build their nest. This is where they'll lay their eggs.

- Different birds build their nests in different shapes and out of different things.

- Blackbirds build their cup-shaped nest out of long grasses and other plant material like twigs, dead leaves and moss. They plaster the inside of their nest with mud, then line it with fine grass.

- Usually only the *female* Blackbird does the nest-building.

- She's very picky about the materials she chooses. When a Blackbird builds her nest in our hedge, we watch her peck at lots of different bits of grass before she finds some that she takes for her nest. She also turfs out lots of things from our gutter to find exactly the right kind of mud, moss or leaves that she's looking for.

- Female Blackbirds can get very territorial at this time of year. If a Song Thrush or a Blackbird that's not her mate lands near to where a female is building her nest, she'll shoo it away. Sometimes she even ends up fighting to get it off her patch.

- When her nest is finished, the female Blackbird lays a clutch of up to six pale blue-green speckled eggs in it.

Chiffchaff

Who's Calling?

Darling, oh darling
Hark! Spring is here!
The Chiffchaff is back
With his call of good cheer.
Darling, oh darling
Hark! Loud and clear
The Chiffchaff is singing
What joy to the ear!

Darling, oh darling
It's driving me potty!
The same two shrill notes
For three months on the trotty.
What does it look like
This bird, is it spotty?
I've a good mind to fill it
Full of lead shotty!

*Darling, oh darling
Hark! It's gone quiet.
Not a chiff, not a chaff
Just a breathtaking riot
Of silence. Allelujah!
What a relief!
That birdbrain's been giving me
Serious grief.*

BIRD BOX

Common name	Chiffchaff
Scientific name	*Phylloscopus collybita*
Family	Leaf Warblers | Phylloscopidae
Order	Passerines | Passeriformes
Class	Birds | Aves
Phylum	Vertebrates | Chordata
Kingdom	Animals | Animalia
Length	11cm

EGGHEAD

- Some British birds live their whole life in Britain. They're our resident birds.

- Other birds are migrant visitors. Our migrant visitors spend some of the year in Britain, and the rest of the year somewhere else.

- Most of our Chiffchaffs are migrant visitors. They spend the winter months in North Africa or southern Europe, where it's warmer. Then they fly back to Britain in the spring to breed.

- These Chiffchaffs arrive here as early as the end of February. They're one of the first migrants of the year to arrive and they start singing straightaway. So hearing your first Chiffchaff is a real sign that winter is nearly behind us and spring is – literally – in the air.

- Chiffchaffs are called Chiffchaffs because of their song, which simply goes 'chiff-chaff', repeated over and over and over again.

- Like most of our birds, it's only the male Chiffchaff that sings. He likes to sing high up in a tree – for three months or more.

- 'Birdbrain' is a word people use to mean someone stupid. But birds are very far from being stupid. Their brain can work out how to migrate across entire continents and oceans – something we can only do with maps and satnavs to guide us!

Greenfinch

Colour Coded

Have you seen
The green
Of my plumage?
Yes, *you!*
Have you clocked
My blocks
Of yellow?

Have you seen
The sheen
Of my green?
It all means
That I
Am a top-notch
Fellow!

Yes it means
That my genes
Are supreme
This you glean
At a glance
I do not need
To bellow.

A juvenile Greenfinch

BIRD BOX

Common name	Greenfinch
Scientific name	*Chloris chloris*
Family	Finches | Fringillidae
Order	Passerines | Passeriformes
Class	Birds | Aves
Phylum	Vertebrates | Chordata
Kingdom	Animals | Animalia
Length	14–15cm

EGGHEAD

- Birds are the only animals on earth that are covered in feathers. They inherited these from their dinosaur ancestors 150 million years ago or more.

- A bird's feathers are known as its plumage. This word comes from the Latin word *pluma*, which means 'feather'.

- A bird's plumage looks different at different times in its life.

- For example, the plumage of a juvenile (young) male Greenfinch is pale browny-green with streaky patterns. But the plumage of an adult male Greenfinch is olive green with striking yellow flashes on its wings and tail.

- In spring, these green and yellow colours are even more bright and intense. The adult male Greenfinch is then in its breeding plumage, which you can see in the photo above. The better the breeding plumage, the more attractive the male is to females.

- Most birds change from their winter plumage to their breeding plumage by moulting. When they moult, birds lose one set of feathers and grow another set.

- But Greenfinches change their plumage in a different way. The pale tips of their feathers get rubbed away over the winter to reveal the brighter colours underneath.

Pheasant

On Guard!

NO!
Don't you dare!
Off you go!
This is *mine!*

I said NO!
Are you deaf?
You try that
One more time

I will come at you
Peck at you
Jab at you
FIE!

This here's
My turf.
Keep out!
Goodbye.

BIRD BOX

Common name	Pheasant
Scientific name	*Phasianus colchicus*
Family	Pheasants & allies | Phasianidae
Order	Gamebirds | Galliformes
Class	Birds | Aves
Phylum	Vertebrates | Chordata
Kingdom	Animals | Animalia
Length	65–90cm (male)

EGGHEAD

- In spring, male birds spend a lot of time marking and defending the area they've chosen to be their breeding territory. This territory is the place where they'll mate, nest and feed their young.

- Protecting territory is a very important job. Most birds do this by singing and by displaying. When they display, birds often puff up their feathers. This makes them look bigger and more threatening. Another tactic is to just chase their rivals away.

- But Pheasants are different. If the loud calls and threat displays of a male Pheasant don't get rid of a rival, things turn violent. Very violent.

- Male Pheasants have sharp spurs on the back of their legs. They attack each other with these and with their claws.

- They also leap up and bite each other's wattles. (Wattles are the bright red folds of skin that dangle down under male Pheasants' eyes. You can see them clearly opposite.)

- The fighting can be very aggressive and can last up to an hour. The Pheasants don't generally fight to the death. Instead, the intruder usually backs down and leaves the territory.

- Pheasants are mainly farmland birds, but they do sometimes visit gardens.

Swallow

Intercontinental

I remember, I remember
The place where I was born
I remember, I remember
This porch, the path, the lawn
I remember, I remember
That oak, bare and forlorn
I remember, I remember
Farmers' fields of burgeoning corn.

I remember, I remember
This church, its pointy spire
I remember, I remember
The singing of the choir
I remember, I remember
Here's where I became a flier
I remember, I remember
Congregating on that wire.

I remember, I remember
Patchwork gardens down below
I remember, I remember
Matchbox houses row on row
I remember, I remember
As my chicks born here will know
The landmarks and the landscape
Before it's time to go.

We remember, we remember
We are back, we have returned
From beyond the equator
As the seasons they have turned
We have left the parched savannahs
Where the sun beat down and burned
And arrived in muddy England
To take up where we adjourned.

BIRD BOX

Common name	Swallow
Scientific name	*Hirundo rustica*
Family	Swallows & Martins | Hirundinidae
Order	Passerines | Passeriformes
Class	Birds | Aves
Phylum	Vertebrates | Chordata
Kingdom	Animals | Animalia
Length	19cm

EGGHEAD

• Like Chiffchaffs (page 18), Swallows are migrant visitors that come to Britain to breed. They fly from thousands of miles away and arrive in March and April. Year after year, each Swallow flies back here to the same place that it was born.

• We know about Swallow migration now. But it used to be a mystery. Some people thought Swallows spent autumn and winter hibernating in caves, or even underwater.

• In 1912 we finally discovered that what they actually do is migrate, to southern Africa. We worked this out because someone in South Africa found a Swallow that had been ringed in England.

• Ringing involves putting a metal or plastic identifying ring on a bird's leg. We've discovered lots about birds thanks to ringing, including where they migrate to and how long they live.

• Nowadays we can also attach high-tech devices such as GPS tags and data loggers to birds. These give us much more detailed information about migration.

• We know now that birds find their way when they're migrating using a mixture of the sun, the stars, the earth's magnetic field and things they see below. Some birds even use their sense of smell!

• This poem was inspired by a poem by Thomas Hood called 'I Remember, I Remember'.

Great Spotted Woodpecker

Zero-Concussion Percussion

'Knock, knock!'
      'Who's there?'
'Woodpecker.'
      'Spotted!'   'WHERE?'

Skull slung
      In a sling
So drumming doesn't
      Smash the thing.

BIRD BOX

Common name	Great Spotted Woodpecker
Scientific name	*Dendrocopos major*
Family	Woodpeckers | Picidae
Order	Woodpeckers etc. | Piciformes
Class	Birds | Aves
Phylum	Vertebrates | Chordata
Kingdom	Animals | Animalia
Length	23–24cm

EGGHEAD

- Claiming and defending territory are very important jobs for birds. One of the main ways they do this is by singing (see the Chiffchaff on page 18). But Great Spotted Woodpeckers don't do it by singing. Instead, they drum.

- Usually it's only our male birds that sing. But both male and female Great Spotted Woodpeckers drum.

- They create their drumming sound by hammering their strong beak against the branch or trunk of a tree. They often choose dead or hollow trunks and branches because these make a louder sound.

- Great Spotted Woodpeckers drum very fast – up to 40 times per second. That's way too fast for us humans to hear the individual blows.

- They also hammer on trees to hollow out a hole in which they'll nest. Both the male and the female create this nest hole, which is about 30cm deep.

- The force created when a woodpecker's beak hits wood is huge. If we hit our heads that hard we'd be seriously injured, or even killed.

- But the woodpecker has several special design features that allow it to hammer without getting hurt. One of these is its hyoid bone. This bone forms a sort of sling around the skull. It acts like a seat belt for the bird's head and so protects it from harm.

Cuckoo

Hark the Herald

Time was, we were important
Time was, folk wrote to the press
To report that they had heard us
Nowadays they just have to guess

For who on earth can hear us
Above the perpetual roar?
Oh how I long for the way of life
We used to enjoy before

Before juggernauts, vans and lorries
Motorbikes, cars and planes
Before rumblings and revvings and whinings
Throbbed incessantly through our brains

Oh bring back the old days, bring them back do
They were so much better than this
A life pre-petrol engine
A life of acoustic bliss.

BIRD BOX

Common name	Cuckoo
Scientific name	*Cuculus canorus*
Family	Cuckoos | Cuculidae
Order	Cuckoos | Cuculiformes
Class	Birds | Aves
Phylum	Vertebrates | Chordata
Kingdom	Animals | Animalia
Length	33–35cm

EGGHEAD

- Like Chiffchaffs (page 18) and Swallows (page 24), Cuckoos are migrant visitors. They arrive in Britain from Central Africa in April.

- Hearing the first Cuckoo of the year has been important to people here for hundreds of years. The English composer Delius even wrote a piece of music called 'On Hearing the First Cuckoo in Spring'.

- There's a tradition of people writing to *The Times* newspaper when they heard their first Cuckoo. It would cheer up the whole country to read that a Cuckoo had been heard, so summer wouldn't be far away.

- But the noise from modern traffic, building sites and so on has made it harder and harder for us to hear birds singing.

- And harder and harder for birds to hear each other too. Which is a serious problem, as birds sing and call for important reasons, such as to find a mate, to defend their territory and to warn of danger.

- Have you ever heard a Cuckoo? As the name suggests, it goes: 'cuck-coo'. It's only the male that sings this, to attract a female he can mate with.

- Unlike Chiffchaffs and Swallows, Cuckoos don't stay here long. Lots of Cuckoos set off back to Africa as early as June, leaving a different species of bird to sit on their eggs and raise their young.

Magpie

Daylight Robbery

I spy a Magpie
My oh my!
With a swagger in his gait
And a glint in his eye
A head full of tricks
A nest full of bling:
Three coins, a bottle top
And my gold ring.

BIRD BOX

Common name	Magpie
Scientific name	*Pica pica*
Family	Crows | Corvidae
Order	Passerines | Passeriformes
Class	Birds | Aves
Phylum	Vertebrates | Chordata
Kingdom	Animals | Animalia
Length	45–50cm

EGGHEAD

- Many Magpies are kleptomaniacs. That means they steal lots of things, especially shiny things, which they often take back to their nest.

- The Italian composer Rossini wrote an opera called 'The Thieving Magpie' in which a Magpie does just that.

- We don't know for certain why Magpies like shiny objects. Some people think the male Magpie collects them to attract a mate.

- Magpies also steal eggs and nestlings from other birds' nests. It's easy to understand why they do that. They steal them to eat them.

- Many people think it's unlucky to see just one Magpie, so they always look around to see if they can spot at least one more.

- Do you know the rhyme about Magpies that begins: 'One for sorrow, Two for joy, Three for a girl, Four for a boy'?

- Sometimes you'll hear a Magpie without being able to see it. Like Cuckoos (page 28) and Chiffchaffs (page 18), Magpies are easy to identify by the sound they make. They don't sing prettily. They cackle. You can hear what Magpies sound like – and what all the other birds in this book sound like too – at my website. Go to www.theBigBuzz.biz and click on the picture of this book.

Rook

Conviviality

Caw, Caw
What's life for, for?
On your tod, tod
Would be odd, odd
We live loud, loud
In a crowd, crowd
Day is done, done
Sleep as one, one.

Caw, Caw
What's life for, for?
From the crown, crown
We look down, down
Build our nest, nest
With the rest, rest
Way up high, high
Hue and cry, cry.

Caw, Caw
What's life for, for?
Caw, Caw
Make a racket, racket
Caw, Caw
Then you'll crack it, crack it
Caw, Caw
Lay or back it, back it.

Lots of nests in a rookery

BIRD BOX

Common name	Rook
Scientific name	*Corvus frugilegus*
Family	Crows | Corvidae
Order	Passerines | Passeriformes
Class	Birds | Aves
Phylum	Vertebrates | Chordata
Kingdom	Animals | Animalia
Length	43–48cm

EGGHEAD

• Some birds are loners. A Robin (page 96), for example, will usually shoo off any other Robin – except its mate – that dares to show up. And a male Pheasant may well fight another male Pheasant that comes near (see page 22).

• But other birds like company. They're social. Rooks are social. *Very* social. They hang out in big flocks with as many as 18,000 other Rooks. They eat together, roost (that means sleep) together and nest together.

• Rooks make a lot of racket. They brashly 'caw caw' to each other all day long.

• They build their nests near to one another in the tops of tall trees. This creates what's known as a rookery.

• My first school trip, when I was five years old, was a short walk to a nearby rookery. It was a bustling, noisy place, and it made a big impression on me.

• I've kept an eye out for Rooks' nests ever since. They're quite common and easy to spot. I've seen them in groups of tall trees deep in the countryside and also right in the middle of towns.

• So next time you see a clump of tall trees, remember to look up and see if you can see a rookery there.

Mistle Thrush

**Incubation
Incubation
Incubation**

Got to keep them warm
Got to keep them warm
I'm sitting on my eggs in my nest
In my nest.

It's working like a charm
Working like a charm
I'm sitting on my eggs in my nest
In my nest.

In the hawthorn
In the hawthorn
I'm sitting on my eggs in my nest
In my nest.

Keep them safe from harm
Keep them safe from harm
I'm sitting on my eggs in my nest
In my nest.

There's a cat on the lawn!
A cat on the lawn!
And I'm sitting on my eggs in my nest
In my nest.

Hubby's sounding the alarm
Sounding the alarm
And I'm sitting on my eggs in my nest
In my nest.

Feeling careworn
Feeling careworn
Sitting on my eggs in my nest
In my nest.

Try to keep calm
Try to keep calm
While I'm sitting on my eggs in my nest
In my nest.

Stifling a yawn
Stifling a yawn
As I'm sitting on my eggs in my nest
In my nest.

It's driving me barm-y
Driving me barm-y
Sitting on my eggs in my nest
In my nest.

Hurry up and hatch!
Hurry up and hatch!
So I don't have to flippin' well
Sit on my eggs in my nest
ANY MORE!

BIRD BOX

Common name	Mistle Thrush
Scientific name	*Turdus viscivorus*
Family	Chats & Thrushes | Turdidae
Order	Passerines | Passeriformes
Class	Birds | Aves
Phylum	Vertebrates | Chordata
Kingdom	Animals | Animalia
Length	27cm

EGGHEAD

- All bird species lay eggs. A female Mistle Thrush lays up to five speckled eggs in the cup-shaped nest she's built in a tree or bush.

- For birds' eggs to develop, they have to be kept warm. This is called incubation.

- Only the *female* Mistle Thrush incubates her eggs. She does so for about two weeks. This is called the incubation period. After this, the eggs hatch.

- The Mistle Thrush incubates her eggs by sitting on them, covering them – as most of our birds do – with her brood patch. The brood patch is an area of skin on her tummy that has lost its feathers. This means her body heat can pass straight through her skin and keep her eggs nicely warm.

- While she's on her nest, the Mistle Thrush is in danger. She might be attacked – perhaps by a cat or a bird of prey.

- Whenever she leaves the nest to find food, her eggs are in danger. They might be stolen by a Magpie (page 30) or a squirrel.

- During the incubation period, the male Mistle Thrush guards the territory, warns his mate of any threats and attacks other birds that go near the nest.

Oystercatcher

The Great Escape

Pipping
And
Chipping
And
Nipping
And
Snipping

Picking
And
Cricking
And
Ricking
And
Kicking

Twisting
And
Turning
And
Tugging
Yip-
peee!!

I've
Done it
I've
Made it
I'm
Out
I'm FREE!

An adult Oystercatcher on its scrape

A young Oystercatcher chick

BIRD BOX

Common name	Oystercatcher
Scientific name	*Haematopus ostralegus*
Family	Oystercatchers | Haematopodidae
Order	Waders, Gulls etc. | Charadriiformes
Class	Birds | Aves
Phylum	Vertebrates | Chordata
Kingdom	Animals | Animalia
Length	43cm

EGGHEAD

- Most British birds build a nest to lay their eggs in. Oystercatchers don't. Instead, they just make a shallow dip in the ground, called a scrape, and lay their camouflaged eggs there.

- Male and female Oystercatchers take it in turns to incubate their eggs. After about 27 days, the chicks inside the eggs will have developed enough to be ready to hatch.

- Hatching is hard work for all birds, and they need specialist equipment to do it.

- From inside the egg, the curled-up chick pips its first hole in the shell with its egg tooth. The egg tooth is a little horn on the top of the bill. The chick uses it like a pick or a hammer to hack at the egg shell.

- The chick needs to push hard against the top of the shell. It can do this because it has a specially strong hatching muscle in the back of its neck.

- The chick pips and nibbles and pushes at the hole making it bigger and bigger. When it's big enough, the chick clambers out.

- The hatching muscle and the egg tooth both disappear a few days after the chick has hatched.

Mistle Thrush

Parental Responsibility

Flitting back and forwards
Back and forwards to the nest
The nestlings all need feeding
So there's little time to rest

From dawn to dusk it's to and fro
To and fro in turns
Bringing brimming beakfuls
Of grubs and little worms

Day in, day out, it's back and forth
Back and forth they fly
The worms they bring back bigger
As the weeks go by

The squawking's getting louder
Soon be time to fledge
I'll miss this young thrush family
In my garden hedge.

Nestlings getting older

BIRD BOX

Common name	Mistle Thrush
Scientific name	*Turdus viscivorus*
Family	Chats & Thrushes | Turdidae
Order	Passerines | Passeriformes
Class	Birds | Aves
Phylum	Vertebrates | Chordata
Kingdom	Animals | Animalia
Length	27cm

EGGHEAD

- When they hatch, some birds are already quite developed. For example, Oystercatcher chicks (page 36) are covered in downy feathers and can see, walk and even run straightaway. They leave their nest within a day after they hatch. This sort of bird is called precocial.

- But most birds are quite undeveloped when they hatch. They have no feathers, are blind, can hardly move and are totally dependent on their parents. These birds are called altricial.

- Mistle Thrushes – like all our garden birds – are altricial. One thing an altricial chick can do straightaway is gape. Gaping means opening its beak wide. This makes its parents start to feed it.

- Altricial chicks need to be fed lots and lots of food, because they have lots and lots of growing to do.

- With up to five nestlings in a brood, Mistle Thrush parents have to make hundreds of trips to their nest each day to bring back enough food for all their young.

- As the nestlings get older and more developed, they start calling to encourage their parents to keep feeding them.

- About two weeks after they hatch, Mistle Thrush chicks have finally developed enough to be able to leave their nest. Leaving the nest is called fledging.

Summer

Wren	42
Herring Gull	44
Hen Harrier	46
Blue Tit	48
Blackbird	50
Great Tit	52
Swift	54
Buzzard	56
Pied Wagtail	58
House Martin	60
Great Crested Grebe & Mallard	62
Blackbird	66

Wren

The Voice

When
The Wren
Sings
Sings long
Sings loud

    When
    The Wren
    Sings
    Sings strong
    Sings proud

        When
        The Wren
        Sings
        Sings sweet
        Sings true

            When
            The Wren
            Sings
            My heart
            Sings too.

BIRD BOX

Common name	Wren
Scientific name	*Troglodytes troglodytes*
Family	Wrens | Troglodytidae
Order	Passerines | Passeriformes
Class	Birds | Aves
Phylum	Vertebrates | Chordata
Kingdom	Animals | Animalia
Length	9–10cm

EGGHEAD

● The Wren is one of the three tiniest birds in Britain. (The other two are the Goldcrest and the Firecrest.) Although it's tiny, the Wren sings amazingly loudly, and very beautifully.

● It also sings very fast. There are around 56 notes in a 5.2-second burst of Wren song. That's too fast for a human to hear each note.

● We humans create our voice using our larynx (also called our Adam's apple). Birds have a larynx, but they don't use it to create their voice. Instead, their voice organ is their syrinx. We don't have a syrinx.

● Birds generally sing to defend their territory and to attract a mate.

● As with most of our songbirds, it's only the *male* Wren that sings. He sings longest and loudest in the breeding season, which is in spring and early summer.

● The Wren is one of the birds that sings in the dawn chorus. The dawn chorus is a fabulous free concert that starts about an hour before sunrise every morning from March to July. Other birds that sing in the dawn chorus include Blackbirds (page 66), Robins (page 96), finches and thrushes.

● The Wren is our most common breeding bird, so you've a good chance of hearing it sing wherever you are. You can also hear it, and all the other birds in this book, at my website. Go to www.theBigBuzz.biz and click on the picture of this book.

Herring Gull

Air Strikes

A Herring Gull snaffled my ice cream
A Herring Gull nicked his baguette
We were sat on the quayside enjoying a seaside
Day out when the miscreants swept

Down and quite without warning
Made off with our half-eaten fare
One minute I'm holding a cornet
The next, it's up in mid-air

You can't mess with a gull when it's hungry
They're stonkingly big burly things
Screechingly anti-social
Think hoodie with beak, claws and wings

Yes, they're streetwise and canny and cocky
They'll circle then swoop in a trice
So think twice before eating al fresco
By the sea, or you could pay the price.

BIRD BOX

Common name	Herring Gull
Scientific name	*Larus argentatus*
Family	Gulls | Laridae
Order	Waders, Gulls etc. | Charadriiformes
Class	Birds | Aves
Phylum	Vertebrates | Chordata
Kingdom	Animals | Animalia
Length	56–62cm

EGGHEAD

• Some birds are picky eaters and will only eat a particular sort of berry or seed.

• Not Herring Gulls. Herring Gulls will eat just about anything, from fish, mice and other Herring Gulls' chicks to your sandwich, your chips or your ice cream!

• Herring Gulls are big birds, so they can seem very threatening to other, smaller, birds. And when they swoop down to grab our food, they can feel very threatening to us too!

• The well-known screeching seagull sound you hear when you arrive at the seaside is made by Herring Gulls.

• Nowadays you can hear that same sound inland too, in and around rubbish tips (also known as landfill sites). That's because Herring Gulls like eating the food we've thrown away that ends up at landfill sites.

• As the number and size of our landfill sites has grown, so the number of inland Herring Gulls has grown too.

• Meanwhile, the number of Herring Gulls by the seaside has fallen a lot. Scientists aren't sure why this is, but they think it could be because there are a lot fewer fishing boats now. Herring Gulls used to really like eating the small fish that the fishermen didn't want and so threw overboard.

Hen Harrier

A male Hen Harrier

Endangered

Silver shimmer
Heather skimmer

Ring tailer
Air sailor

Grouse catcher
Pipit snatcher

Big dipper
Trip flipper

Sky dancer
Slim chancer

Hope carrier
Hen Harrier.

BIRD BOX

Common name	Hen Harrier
Scientific name	*Circus cyaneus*
Family	Hawks & Eagles | Accipitridae
Order	Hawks, Vultures etc. | Accipitriformes
Class	Birds | Aves
Phylum	Vertebrates | Chordata
Kingdom	Animals | Animalia
Wingspan	100cm (male); 120cm (female)

EGGHEAD

- The males and females of some birds, such as Robins (page 96) or Dunnocks (page 110), look very similar. But the males and females of other birds look very different from each other. Male Hen Harriers look so different from females that for centuries people thought they were two different species. This difference between the sexes is called sexual dimorphism.

- Adult male Hen Harriers are pale grey and are known as silver ghosts. Females are larger and mottled brown. They're known as ringtails, because of the bands on their tail.

- Hen Harriers are extremely agile flyers. Males perform a spectacular acrobatic display called a sky dance.

- However, you'd be very lucky to see a sky dance, because Hen Harriers are very rare. They're our most rare bird of prey.

- Why? Well, Hen Harriers like to spend spring and summer on grouse moors, but many of the people who own these moors don't like Hen Harriers being there, because they eat Red Grouse chicks. So it seems that some owners have Hen Harriers killed, even though killing them is illegal.

- Conservation organisations and campaigners are trying to save the Hen Harrier.

- This poem is a special type of riddle poem. Each line is a kenning, which is a way of describing the bird in two words.

Blue Tit

Homesick

Nest
Is best!
I want me nest
That were best!

It were cosy
And comfy
Now I'm lonely
And grumpy

I want me nest
That were best!
Me nest
Were best!

Here it's louder
And lighter
Busier
And brighter

I want me nest
That were best!
Me nest
Were best!

I were surrounded
By siblings
Fed with succulent
Nibblings

Oh, me nest
Were best!
I want me nest
That were best!

Outdoors ain't
For me
I'd rather
Be

In my nest
That were best!
Oh, me nest
Were best!

Oh give it a rest!
Nest isn't best
Life on the wing
That's the Real Thing!!

BIRD BOX

Common name .... Blue Tit
Scientific name .. *Cyanistes caeruleus*
Family .... Tits | Paridae
Order ..... Passerines | Passeriformes
Class .... Birds | Aves
Phylum .... Vertebrates | Chordata
Kingdom .... Animals | Animalia
Length 11–12cm

EGGHEAD

- A Blue Tit nest is very soft and comfy. That's because it's made mostly out of moss. Blue Tits often build their nest in a nest box.

- A female Blue Tit lays up to 16 eggs. That must make it very cosy in the nest box once all the chicks have hatched.

- When they're about three weeks old, Blue Tit nestlings fledge. That means they leave their nest.

- The parents call to the nestlings from outside the nest box to encourage them to come out. Some of them fly out very eagerly. Others don't.

- I watched the Blue Tit in this photo fledge from the nest box in our garden. It was the very last bird to leave the box. It kept poking its head out of the hole, but it didn't seem to want to actually leave. Its parents kept calling to it and it eventually made its maiden flight – of around six metres to our honeysuckle bush.

- I took this photo straight after it had landed. As you can see, it didn't look too pleased to be in the outside world.

- Do you have a nest box in your garden or school grounds? I thoroughly recommend having one!

Blackbird

Pester Power

Feed me! Feed me!
More, MORE, **MORE**!
Bring me food
That's what you're for!

Feed me! Feed me!
Faster, **FASTER**!
Grubs and seeds
Are what I'm after.

Feed me! Feed me!
Yum, YUM, **YUM**!
Tasty morsels
For my tum.

Feed me! Feed me!
Go, GO, **GO**!
Gee it up
You're way too slow!

Feed me! Feed me!
Can't you see?
I'm STARVING perched here
By this tree.

Feed me! Feed me!
Now, NOW, **NOW**!
DIY?
Don't know how.

Feed me! Feed me!
What the heck
This looks nice
I'll have a peck – **YUCK**!

Feed me! Feed me!
Ooo, what's this?
A sunflower seed?
Mmm … what bliss!

Now I get it!
Easy as pie
I can feed me
So: Bye-bye!

BIRD BOX

Common name . . . . Blackbird
Scientific name . . . . *Turdus merula*
Family . . . Chats & Thrushes | Turdidae
Order . . . . . Passerines | Passeriformes
Class . . . . Birds | Aves
Phylum . . . . Vertebrates | Chordata
Kingdom . . . . Animals | Animalia

Length . . . . 25–28cm (adult)

EGGHEAD

- Blackbird nestlings fledge about two weeks after they hatch.

- Like most altricial birds (see page 39), Blackbird fledglings still need to be fed by their parents. They have a lot of growing and learning to do before they can fend for themselves.

- When they first fledge, Blackbirds only have a very short, stubby tail, and they can't fly. They just sit somewhere sheltered, hiding from predators, waiting for their parents to come and feed them.

- Within a week, the fledglings have developed enough to be able to fly. They then start following their parents around, pestering them and begging them for food.

- Eventually the fledglings start to experiment for themselves. They peck at different things they come across to see if they can eat them.

- By about three weeks after they fledge, the young Blackbirds have learned how to feed and look after themselves.

- If it's early enough in the season, their parents will go off and start another brood. A pair of Blackbirds usually raises two or three broods each year. They often re-use the same nest. But not even half of the eggs the female lays will survive to become fully fledged, independent birds.

Great Tit

A Great Tit in peak condition

Me Time

I'm bedraggled
And befrazzled
Need to rest
My weary head
But I've all these
Gaping mouths
That are demanding
To be fed
They are clamouring
And yammering
Insatiable
In vain
Do I try
To fill them up
They simply **squawk** at me
Again.

I am moulting
Look revolting
Need a decent
Wash and preen
But I haven't
Got a moment
To myself
Inbetween
All my comings
And my goings
Endless sorties
Finding food
For my dearest, darling
Simply starving
Helpless, hapless
Brood.

I'm exhausted
And exasperated
Can't go on
Much longer
But it looks to me
– At last –
As if my babes
Are getting stronger
And smarter
Have worked out
They have to pull their weight
And peck!
Hurrah!
Just in time
I'm about to
Hit the deck.

A Great Tit fledgling clamouring for food

BIRD BOX

Common name	Great Tit
Scientific name	*Parus major*
Family	Tits | Paridae
Order	Passerines | Passeriformes
Class	Birds | Aves
Phylum	Vertebrates | Chordata
Kingdom	Animals | Animalia
Length	14–15cm

EGGHEAD

- Being a parent can be extremely hard work. Especially if, like Great Tits, your chicks are altricial. (See the altricial Mistle Thrushes on page 39.)

- When it hatches, a Great Tit chick weighs about 1.5g. Three weeks later, when it fledges, it weighs up to 26g. To grow that much, that fast, the chick needs to eat a huge amount of food.

- Great Tits usually have between seven and nine chicks in a brood – sometimes even more. During the three weeks the chicks are in their nest, the parents bring them over 10,000 caterpillars to eat.

- The parents also take away from the nest their nestlings' bags of poo, called faecal sacs.

- The parents make hundreds and hundreds of trips in and out of the nest every day. They have hardly any time to look after themselves. Which is why they – like other parent birds – start to look more and more untidy as the weeks wear on.

- The parents' work isn't over when their nestlings fledge. Great Tit fledglings stay close to their parents, demanding to be fed by them, for a few weeks more, until they've learned to feed and look after themselves.

- By this time, parent birds can end up looking very dirty, dishevelled and exhausted!

Swift

Fast

Swift by name
Swift by nature
You're a fly?
You were – I ate yer!

Tell-tale outline
Monochrome
I scythe the sky
My year-round home.

BIRD BOX

Common name . . . . Swift
Scientific name . . . . *Apus apus*
Family . . . . Swifts | Apodidae
Order . . . . Swifts | Apodiformes
Class . . . . Birds | Aves
Phylum . . . . Vertebrates | Chordata
Kingdom . . . . Animals | Animalia
Length .16–17cm

EGGHEAD

- Swifts can fly fast – *very* fast. In 2010, scientists measured them flying at 111.6km per hour (69.3 miles per hour). This made Swifts the fastest birds ever recorded in level flight (not diving with the help of gravity). But that's not their only world record.

- Swifts also spend longer in the air than any other bird. Some Swifts don't touch the ground for ten months at a time. They eat, mate and even sleep whilst flying (also known as being on the wing).

- Swifts eat insects. To catch the insects, Swifts simply fly with their beak wide open – as you can see in this photo – scooping up any that are in their path.

- Swifts are migrant visitors that fly here non-stop from Africa in late April and early May. They can make this 5,000km journey in just five days.

- Swifts have been described as 'the ultimate flying machine'. They can fly so fast, so far and so acrobatically thanks to their long, narrow, swept-back wings and thin body.

- Swifts' wings give them a tell-tale shape in the air, which makes them easy for us to identify.

- A Swift can live for over 20 years. In its lifetime, it flies a distance roughly equal to seven trips to the moon and back.

Buzzard

High Rise

I ride the thermals, Circle, soar

Flapping's such a wasteful bore

I ride the thermals, High up, high

A silent, deadly, aerial spy

I ride the thermals, Wing tips splayed

Preparing for my pinpoint raid

I ride the thermals, Nice and slow

Why so frenetic down below?

BIRD BOX

Common name	Buzzard
Scientific name	*Buteo buteo*
Family	Hawks & Eagles | Accipitridae
Order	Hawks, Vultures etc. | Accipitriformes
Class	Birds | Aves
Phylum	Vertebrates | Chordata
Kingdom	Animals | Animalia
Wingspan	115–130cm

EGGHEAD

- The Buzzard is a very big bird. But I've only seen it as a small fleck high in the sky, circling slowly with its wing tips splayed out.

- The Buzzard likes to circle on rising thermals of hot air.

- It can soar, circle and glide thanks to its special shape: broad wings, slotted wing tips and a wide rounded tail.

- The Buzzard is a bird of prey. When it's circling way up in the sky, it's scanning the land below, hunting for food.

- Buzzards eat live prey such as mammals, reptiles, amphibians and insects. They also eat carrion (dead animals).

- To be able to spot their prey way down on the ground, Buzzards need very acute eyesight. And that's exactly what they have. Their eyesight is around eight times better than ours. It's said that a Buzzard can spot prey as small as a beetle from high up in the sky.

- The Buzzard is now our most common and widespread bird of prey. So look up and keep an eye out where you are for a bird with broad wings that's circling slowly, high in the sky.

Pied Wagtail

The Fidget

Soaring
    Is boring
Circling's
  No fun
I'd rather
  Waggle
    My tail with a
  Gaggle
  Of mates
      In a car park
  Or on a
    Grass verge
Or a field

Or maybe
  If we get the
    Urge
On a football pitch
  Which
  I'm sure you'll
  Agree
Is better
    By far
      Than up in
        A tree

Or worse
      In mid-air
What a curse!
Who'd be there?!

BIRD BOX

Common name .... Pied Wagtail
Scientific name *Motacilla alba yarrellii*
Family .. Pipits & Wagtails | Motacillidae
Order ..... Passerines | Passeriformes
Class .... Birds | Aves
Phylum .... Vertebrates | Chordata
Kingdom .... Animals | Animalia
Length 18cm

EGGHEAD

- Guess why wagtails are called wagtails. Yes, it's because they wag their tail up and down, up and down, up and down when they're on the ground. Which is where they spend a lot of their time.

- Some birds, such as Robins (page 96) and House Sparrows (page 78), can only hop when they're on the ground. But wagtails can walk – and walk fast.

- The Latin scientific name for wagtails originally meant 'little mover'. And if you watch a Pied Wagtail, you'll see what a fidget it is. It spends a lot of time on the ground scurrying in short bursts, first one way then another, with its head jerking to and fro.

- Every now and then it flutter jumps a little way into the air to catch an insect.

- Pied Wagtails aren't loners, they're social birds. You'll often see a small group of them together on a playing field or a car park or some other flat open ground.

- And at dusk you might see *lots* more of them, as hundreds, even thousands, gather to roost (sleep) close to each other in groups of trees.

- In winter they even do this in the very centre of towns and cities, as it's warmer there.

House Martin

FlapChat

Newly fledged, aghast we listen to
The grown-ups spinning yarns from days of yore:
'We numbered then so many, many more.
Filled the summer sky, blocked out the blue.'
Stories, stories while they skim and swoop:
'Like swarms of bees,' they murmur, streaming past.
We chase and race; they conjure up a cast
Of thousands, daring us to loop the loop.
And then they line us up on strings of wire
And start to tell of journeys yet to come
Of seascapes, deserts, plains, and we're struck dumb
Imagining a heat that burns like fire.
How to disentangle truth from lies?
Take a leap of faith into the skies.

BIRD BOX

Common name	House Martin
Scientific name	*Delichon urbicum*
Family	Swallows & Martins | Hirundinidae
Order	Passerines | Passeriformes
Class	Birds | Aves
Phylum	Vertebrates | Chordata
Kingdom	Animals | Animalia
Length	12–13cm

EGGHEAD

- Like Swallows (page 24), House Martins are migrant visitors in the Hirundinidae family that fly here from Africa. They arrive in spring to build their nests and breed.

- Swifts (page 54) do this too. Swifts look quite like House Martins and Swallows, but they actually belong in a different family, called the Apodidae family.

- House Martins fly *very* acrobatically. They can't fly as fast as Swifts (the world record holders), but they still fly pretty fast – around 80km per hour (50 miles per hour). They only come down to the ground to pick up mud for their nest. They collect between 700 and 1,500 mud pellets to make their nest.

- House Martins like to nest around other House Martins. This means it can get quite hectic at their nesting sites, with lots and lots of birds swooping around very quickly.

- Before they set off on their long flight back to Africa in the autumn, House Martins often gather together on telegraph wires. Swallows do this too.

- When I was young, there were many more House Martins, Swallows and Swifts in Britain than there are now. Their numbers have been falling for decades. You can help them by putting up specially shaped nest boxes.

- This poem is a special sort of poem. It has 14 lines and is called a sonnet.

Great Crested Grebe & Mallard

Different Strokes

They're dumpy and they waddle
And they quack a load of twaddle
Do we have to share our lake
With all these ducks, for heaven's sake?

        They're skinny as a whippet
        And have you seen their poncey tippet?
        Do we have to share our lake
        With snotty grebes, for heaven's sake?

They can't dive, they only dabble
They're a raucous rowdy rabble
Do we have to share our lake
With all these ducks, for heaven's sake?

        They're so stuck up, so high brow
        Think they own this place somehow
        Do we have to share our lake
        With snotty grebes, for heaven's sake?

Let's face it, they are dweebs
And we are cultured Crested Grebes
Do we have to share our lake
With all these ducks, for heaven's sake?

        Their chicks ride piggyback
        Too posh to paddle – and to quack
        Do we have to share our lake
        With snotty grebes, for heaven's sake?

They wouldn't know a fish
If it were served up on a dish
Do we have to share our lake
With all these ducks, for heaven's sake?

        Big deal: they swim underwater
        Where they massacre and slaughter
        Do we have to share our lake
        With snotty grebes, for heaven's sake?

**YES, YOU DO!
GET ON WITH IT!**

BIRD BOX

Common name ....Great Crested Grebe
Scientific name ... *Podiceps cristatus*
Family .... Grebes | Podicipedidae
Order...... Grebes | Podicipediformes
Class .... Birds | Aves
Phylum .... Vertebrates | Chordata
Kingdom .... Animals | Animalia

Length................... 46–51cm

BIRD BOX

Common name ....Mallard
Scientific name .. *Anas platyrhynchos*
Family .... Swans, Geese & Ducks | Anatidae
Order......... Wildfowl | Anseriformes
Class .... Birds | Aves
Phylum .... Vertebrates | Chordata
Kingdom .... Animals | Animalia

Length................... 50–65cm

Great Crested Grebe courtship

Great Crested Grebe & Mallard

An up-ended female and male Mallard

EGGHEAD

- You may see grebes and ducks on the same lake, but they each keep themselves very much to themselves.

- The Great Crested Grebe looks very elegant. It has a long slender neck, a two-tone tippet (a ruff) and a pointy bill, which it uses to catch fish.

- Mallards are our most common duck. They are quite chunky and have a broad, flattened bill. They don't fish. Instead, they dabble. That means they move their bill around in shallow water, filtering out tiny plants and animals to eat.

- Great Crested Grebes perform very complex and beautiful courtship rituals which include a head-shaking ceremony and presenting each other with offerings. Mallards sometimes don't bother with courtship at all. They can be very uncouth when it comes to mating.

- Great Crested Grebes live almost entirely on (and under!) water. They are expert divers and can stay underwater for quite some time. Mallards don't dive. Instead they just up-end themselves to find food below the water's surface. And on land, they waddle.

- Great Crested Grebes carry their chicks around with them on their back. Mallards don't. Mallard ducklings have to swim by themselves.

- Mallards quack. Grebes don't.

Blackbird

Taking the Heat

Phew! What a scorcher
Scorcher, scorcher
Phew! What a scorcher
I'm well hot!

Phew! What a scorcher
Scorcher, scorcher
Phew! What a scorcher
Cool I'm not!

Phew! What a scorcher
Scorcher, scorcher
Phew! What a scorcher
Catch some rays

Phew! What a scorcher
Scorcher, scorcher
Phew! What a scorcher
In a daze

Phew! What a scorcher
Scorcher, scorcher
Phew! What a scorcher
All hang loose

Phew! What a scorcher
Scorcher, scorcher
Phew! What a –
Sun's gone in
Vamoose!

BIRD BOX

Common name	Blackbird
Scientific name	*Turdus merula*
Family	Chats & Thrushes | Turdidae
Order	Passerines | Passeriformes
Class	Birds | Aves
Phylum	Vertebrates | Chordata
Kingdom	Animals | Animalia
Length	25–28m

EGGHEAD

● On a hot day, a Blackbird often chooses a sunny spot and flops down with its beak open, its wings spread out and its feathers splayed – just like this one is doing here. This is called sunning.

● Why do Blackbirds do it? No-one knows for sure, but here are some possible explanations.

● Like most birds, Blackbirds have a gland on their back that produces preen oil. This oil helps keep their feathers clean, flexible and waterproof. Scientists think that sunning may help the preen oil to spread across the Blackbirds' feathers.

● Harmful parasites live on birds' skin and in their feathers. Scientists think that hot sun may drive these parasites to the surface. This would make it easier for a Blackbird to remove them when it preens (see page 79), which it often does straight after sunning.

● Of course another reason Blackbirds flop down like this when it's hot may quite simply be that, like us, they enjoy sunbathing!

● We *do* know why Blackbirds keep their beaks open when they're sunning. Being black, a Blackbird absorbs lots of heat. Birds can't sweat, so to keep themselves as cool as possible when sunning, they hold their beak open and pant instead.

● Some other birds, such as Wrens (page 42) and Robins (page 96), like sunning too. Have you seen any?

Autumn

Long-tailed Tit	70
Grey Heron	72
Feral Pigeon	74
Chaffinch	76
House Sparrow	78
Linnet	80
Little Owl	82
Kingfisher	84
Greylag Goose	86
Song Thrush	88
Dipper	90
Fieldfare	92

Long-tailed Tit

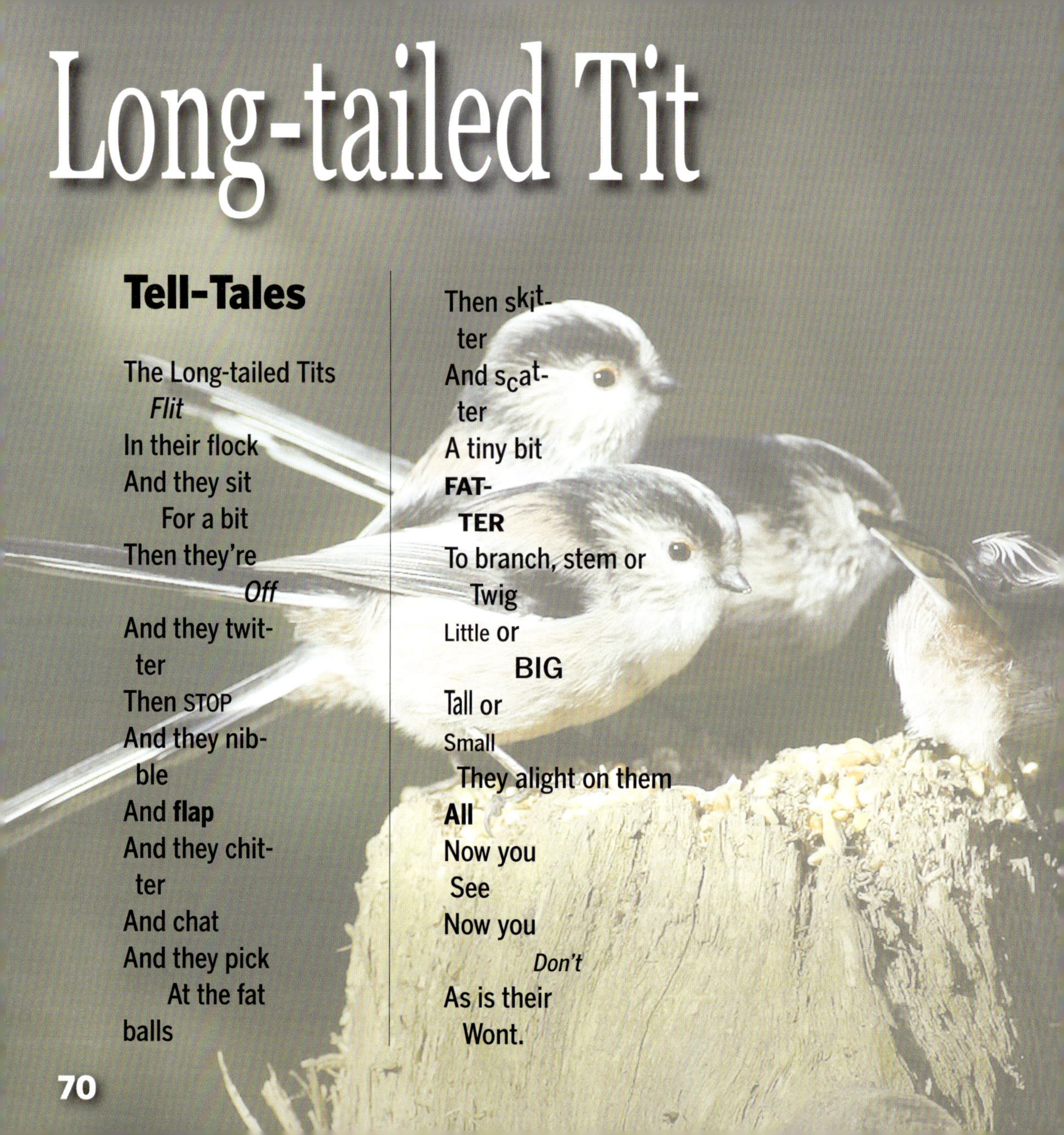

Tell-Tales

The Long-tailed Tits
  Flit
In their flock
And they sit
  For a bit
Then they're
    Off
And they twit-
  ter
Then STOP
And they nib-
  ble
And **flap**
And they chit-
  ter
And chat
And they pick
   At the fat
balls

Then skit-
  ter
And scat-
  ter
A tiny bit
FAT-
TER
To branch, stem or
  Twig
Little or
    BIG
Tall or
Small
  They alight on them
All
Now you
  See
Now you
    Don't
As is their
  Wont.

BIRD BOX

Common name	Long-tailed Tit
Scientific name	*Aegithalos caudatus*
Family	Long-tailed Tits | Aegithalidae
Order	Passerines | Passeriformes
Class	Birds | Aves
Phylum	Vertebrates | Chordata
Kingdom	Animals | Animalia
Length	14cm

EGGHEAD

- We have many different tits in Britain, including Blue Tits (page 48), Great Tits (page 52) and Coal Tits. They all belong to the Paridae family.

- You'd think that the Long-tailed Tit would also belong to the Paridae family. But it doesn't. That's because the Long-tailed Tit isn't actually a tit at all.

- The Long-tailed Tit belongs to the Aegithalidae family. It's the only British bird in that family.

- You'd also think that the Long-tailed Tit would have a long tail. And it does! Its tail is longer than its body.

- Long-tailed Tits often fly around in small flocks, landing one after the next in nearby branches. They stay for just a few moments and then set off again, one by one.

- Even when they're perched, Long-tailed Tits always look very fidgety as they flick their long tails a lot. They do this to help them keep their balance.

- I can tell when Long-tailed Tits have arrived in my garden because I hear them excitedly chitter-chattering to one another. Yes, they're chatter-boxes as well as fidget-bottoms!

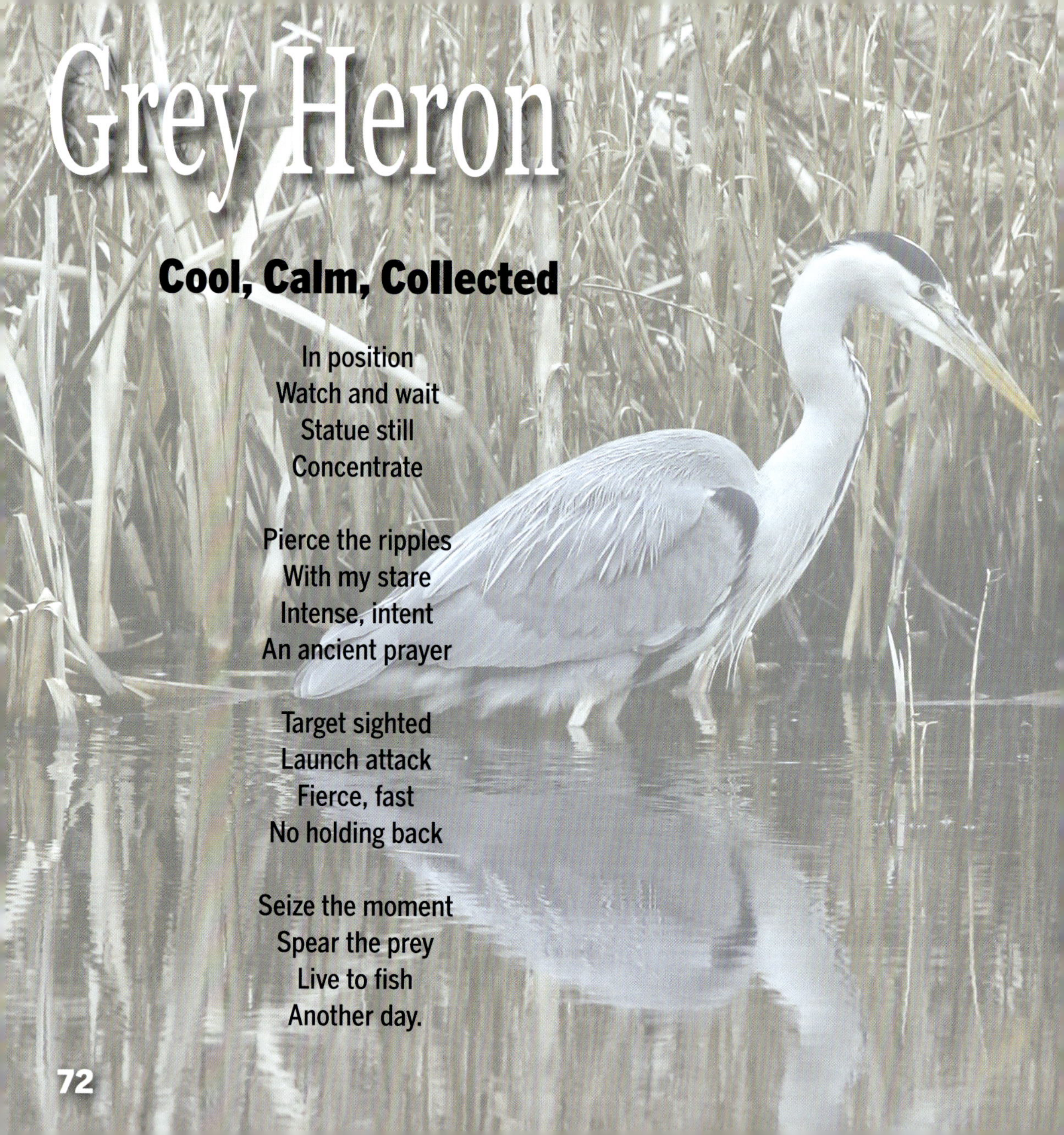

Grey Heron

Cool, Calm, Collected

In position
Watch and wait
Statue still
Concentrate

Pierce the ripples
With my stare
Intense, intent
An ancient prayer

Target sighted
Launch attack
Fierce, fast
No holding back

Seize the moment
Spear the prey
Live to fish
Another day.

BIRD BOX

Common name	Grey Heron
Scientific name	*Ardea cinerea*
Family	Bitterns & Herons | Ardeidae
Order	Egrets, Herons etc. | Ciconiiformes
Class	Birds | Aves
Phylum	Vertebrates | Chordata
Kingdom	Animals | Animalia
Length	90–98cm

EGGHEAD

- Many birds – such as Long-tailed Tits (page 70) and Pied Wagtails (page 58) – are fidgets. They're always flitting or scurrying around.

- The Grey Heron isn't like that. It stays stock still for minutes, even hours, on end.

- Why? Because it's a hunter, and its method of hunting is to be very still, very patient and very quiet.

- It stands by or in water, waiting for its prey – usually fish – to come within reach.

- A successful hunter needs to be able to move very quickly and have a deadly weapon. When the Grey Heron spots a fish coming close, it makes a super-fast lunge and stabs the fish with its long beak, which is as sharp as a dagger.

- You can tell a lot about what birds eat from the shape of their bill. The Bullfinch's short bill (page 106) has very sharp cutting edges that can snip buds off trees. Birds of prey (pages 46, 56, 104) have sharp, hooked bills that are good at tearing the flesh of the animals they catch.

- The Grey Heron is one of the biggest birds in Britain.

Feral Pigeon

Putting the Moves On

I bow down before you
My beak at your feet
Please be mine
I beg, I entreat.

I bow down before you
I bill and I coo
You'd be mad not to have me
My love is true.

I bow down before you
I'd help build our nest
Can't you tell from the feathers
Plumped up on my chest?

I bow down before you
I'd be a great catch
You'll be glad you chose me
When you see our chicks hatch.

I bow down before you
No, don't turn away!
Ah well – I'll have to start over
I've got all day …

[Repeat this poem from the beginning – over and over again.]

BIRD BOX

Common name	Feral Pigeon
Scientific name	*Columba livia*
Family	Pigeons | Columbidae
Order	Pigeons & Doves | Columbiformes
Class	Birds | Aves
Phylum	Vertebrates | Chordata
Kingdom	Animals | Animalia
Length	33cm

EGGHEAD

- Most of our birds breed in spring and early summer. Feral Pigeons are different. They breed all year round.

- To be able to breed, a bird needs to find a mate. One way a male bird attracts a mate is by putting on a courtship display.

- The male Feral Pigeon's courtship display includes him making a cooing sound while bowing down in front of the female with his chest feathers plumped up.

- The female often seems unimpressed and walks or flies away. But the male doesn't give up. Instead, he follows her and tries again. And again. And again!

- Once a male Feral Pigeon has persuaded a female to be his mate, a nest needs to be built. The male brings nesting material (mainly twigs) to the nest site and the female piles it up into a higgledy-piggledy nest.

- Feral Pigeons like being in the same sorts of places as we do, from farms in the countryside to parks, streets, railway stations and squares right in the middle of towns. Their favourite nesting sites include the ledges of buildings.

- So wherever you are, you may well see Feral Pigeon courtship behaviour, and their untidy nests, just about any month of the year.

Chaffinch

Bath Time!

Splish and splash
Splish and splash
Mustn't linger
Got to dash
Dribble water
Down my back
Flick through feathers
(There's a knack)
Dance those droplets
Splish, splosh, splash
Shiver me dry
Done! In a flash!

BIRD BOX

Common name	Chaffinch
Scientific name	*Fringilla coelebs*
Family	Finches | Fringillidae
Order	Passerines | Passeriformes
Class	Birds | Aves
Phylum	Vertebrates | Chordata
Kingdom	Animals | Animalia
Length	15cm

EGGHEAD

- All birds take very good care of their feathers. Their lives depend on their feathers being in good condition.

- Bathing is one of the ways birds look after their feathers. Bathing helps to keep feathers clean and to remove parasites.

- Most birds bathe in water. Some bathe in dust. Some, like House Sparrows (page 78), bathe in water and then bathe in dust.

- Chaffinches bathe in water. They have a set technique for bathing. It doesn't take long. They stand in shallow water and fluff up their feathers. They dip their head in so the water flows down their back, and they flick their wings to create a shower.

- Then they shake off as much water as possible and go and find somewhere to dry off.

- After they've bathed, birds generally preen (see page 79).

- Have you got a bird bath in your garden? Having one helps your local birds keep clean and healthy. And you get to see birds bathing close up. You can find out what makes a good bird bath, and the best place to put it, at my website. Go to www.theBigBuzz.biz and click on the picture of this book.

House Sparrow

Spick and Span

To be able to fly
And to keep warm and dry
I have to look after my feathers
    Cheep! Cheep!
I have to look after them well.

So my daily routine
Is to thoroughly preen
For I have to look after my feathers
    Cheep! Cheep!
I have to look after them well.

I oil them with care
(And with avian flair)
Yes I have to look after my feathers
    Cheep! Cheep!
I have to look after them well.

And my barbs I zip
From the base to the tip
For I have to look after my feathers
    Cheep! Cheep!
I have to look after them well.

I'm a bird – I'm unique!
An evolutionary peak
So I have to look after my feathers
    Cheep! Cheep!
I have to look after them well.

My feathers are key
They're what make me *me*
So I always look after my feathers
    Cheep! Cheep!
Coz they look after me so well.
    Cheep! Cheep! Cheep!

A well-preened House Sparrow

BIRD BOX

Common name .... House Sparrow
Scientific name ... *Passer domesticus*
Family .... Sparrows | Passeridae
Order ..... Passerines | Passeriformes
Class .... Birds | Aves
Phylum .... Vertebrates | Chordata
Kingdom .... Animals | Animalia
Length 14–15cm

EGGHEAD

- Scientists have worked out that birds evolved over millions of years from feathered dinosaurs called theropods. Today, birds are the only animals on the planet that have feathers.

- Feathers are made of keratin – the same thing that our hair and nails are made of. Birds spend a lot of time every day keeping their feathers in good condition. They do this by bathing (see page 77) and by preening.

- When birds preen, they nibble and stroke their bill along individual feathers. This removes dirt and insect parasites, and also keeps the feathers in shape and in the right place.

- A feather is made up of hundreds of tiny parallel barbs that branch off from each side of the centre. The barbs are linked together by tinier hooked branches called barbules. These work a bit like a zip.

- Any gaps in a feather get zipped back together when the bird passes its beak along it.

- When birds preen, they also spread preen oil (from the preen gland on their back, near their tail) over their feathers. This oil keeps the feathers flexible and waterproof.

- Although House Sparrows are classed as songbirds, they don't really sing. They just cheep.

Linnet

What's in a Name?

'That's a Linnet
Innit?'

'No, it's a Furze Bird
You daft nerd!'

'A Thorn Grey
I'd say.'

'It's a Lint White
Alright?'

'A Gorse Hatcher
You can tell by its stature.'

'A Red-headed Finch
I won't budge an inch!'

'But it eats linseed
Are we all agreed?'

'NO, FLAX!'

'OK, *Pax*!'

BIRD BOX

Common name	Linnet
Scientific name	*Linaria cannabina*
Family	Finches | Fringillidae
Order	Passerines | Passeriformes
Class	Birds | Aves
Phylum	Vertebrates | Chordata
Kingdom	Animals | Animalia
Length	13–14cm

EGGHEAD

• In most British bird books, birds appear with two names. One is the English common name that everyone here recognises. The other is the scientific name, also called the Latin name. That consists of two words. It's the name used and recognised by ornithologists worldwide.

• But many of our birds have more than just one English name. These are names you won't find in standard guidebooks, because they are (or were) only used locally by people in different parts of the country.

• In this poem I've used some local English names for the Linnet. For example, in Northamptonshire the Linnet is called a Furze Bird. In Shropshire, it's a Gorse Hatcher.

• The name Linnet comes from the Latin word for the bird's favourite food, which is *Linum*. But even *Linum* has more than one name in English: 'linseed' and 'flax'.

• The Linnet's scientific name changed recently too, from *Carduelis cannabina* to *Linaria cannabina*.

• Scientific names of birds get changed when we understand more about them and their evolution, often through DNA analysis.

• *Pax* is Latin for 'peace'. It's a word schoolchildren used to use to call for an end to a fight or an argument. And there are plenty of names to argue about here!

Little Owl

Night and Day

Small
And dumpy
Flecked
And plumpy
Perched on a
Stump he
Now lives in this
Country.

BIRD BOX

Common name	Little Owl
Scientific name	*Athene noctua*
Family	Owls | Strigidae
Order	Owls | Strigiformes
Class	Birds | Aves
Phylum	Vertebrates | Chordata
Kingdom	Animals | Animalia
Length	22cm

EGGHEAD

- The Little Owl is our smallest owl. It hasn't been here very long. It was only introduced into England – from continental Europe – in the late 19th century.

- The first breeding pair was recorded in Kent, which is in the south-east of England. They must have liked it there, because the species spread rapidly. Little Owls are now found across England, and in Wales and southern Scotland. But their numbers have been falling since the 1960s.

- Unusually for an owl, the Little Owl often hunts in the daytime. This means we have a better chance of seeing it.

- Its compact, dumpy shape makes it an easy bird to identify.

- Keep an eye out for the tell-tale shape of a Little Owl on a fence post or a tree stump. It likes to perch on these as they make good look-out spots when it's hunting.

- The Little Owl's prey includes beetles, crickets, earthworms and small mammals.

- If you see a Little Owl, let the Little Owl Count know. See 'Over to You' on page 133.

Kingfisher

A Kingfisher on its perch

Streaker

Blink and you'll miss me
Blink and I'm gone
I'm not some stately
Statuesque swan

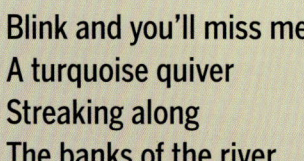

Blink and you'll miss me
A turquoise quiver
Streaking along
The banks of the river.

BIRD BOX

Common name .... Kingfisher
Scientific name .... *Alcedo atthis*
Family ...... Kingfishers | Alcedinidae
Order ..... Kingfishers | Coraciiformes
Class .... Birds | Aves
Phylum .... Vertebrates | Chordata
Kingdom .... Animals | Animalia
Length 16–17cm

EGGHEAD

- If you go walking by a river or a lake, some birds are easy to spot. Swans, geese (page 86) and ducks (page 62), for example, swim in full view. And a Dipper (page 90) will bob up and down on a river boulder.

- Other birds that live near water are much harder to spot. Kingfishers, for example, are really shy.

- If you're very lucky, you might catch a glimpse of a Kingfisher flying fast and low, close to the riverbank. You'll know it's a Kingfisher because of its shimmering turquoise-blue back and wings.

- But its turquoise-blue feathers aren't really blue at all. They just look blue to us because of the way the light shines off them.

- If you're very, very lucky on your walk, you might see a Kingfisher perched on a branch overhanging the river. Maybe it's looking for small fish to eat in the water below. Or maybe it's just dived in and caught one.

- When the Kingfisher is on its perch, you'll probably be able to see its bright orange feathers, as well as its blue ones.

- These orange feathers really *are* orange. The orange colour is created, just like paint colours, by a pigment that's in the feathers. This is how the colours of most British birds' feathers are created.

Greylag Goose

Formation Flying

We could give you the facts and figures:
Air resistance; upwash; drag;
Efficient use of resources
This may or may not be your bag.

Or instead you could go out tonight
And gaze up as we honk overhead
Feel the whoosh we whip up with our wings
Understand with your heart, not your head.

Pink-footed Geese flying in a V-formation

BIRD BOX

Common name .... Greylag Goose
Scientific name .... *Anser anser*
Family .... Swans, Geese & Ducks | Anatidae
Order .... Wildfowl | Anseriformes
Class .... Birds | Aves
Phylum .... Vertebrates | Chordata
Kingdom .... Animals | Animalia
Length.................. 75–90cm

EGGHEAD

- Next time you hear geese honking overhead, look up. You'll see that they're probably flying in a V-formation, with one goose at the front and the others fanning out behind it, creating a V-shape.

- Scientists have worked out the aerodynamics of flying in this formation. They've discovered that it saves the geese lots of energy. So much energy, in fact, that they can fly up to 70% further than if they flew alone.

- This energy saving happens because each goose benefits from what are called upwash vortex fields that are created by the wings of the goose in front of it.

- There are no upwash vortex fields for the goose at the very front. This means it uses lots more energy to fly.

- To make sure the goose at the front doesn't get too exhausted, the geese take it in turns to fly at the head of the V-formation.

- What scientists will never be able to work out, however, is what you *feel* when a flock of geese flies over your head in this formation. Try it and see. It's a very special feeling.

Song Thrush

Real Meal Deal

Oh you fast food junkies
You haven't a clue
How to fend for yourselves
You don't know what to do

You just flock to their feeders
Full of pre-prepared nosh
Fine fancy fare
All hygienic and posh

Your nuts are pre-shelled
Your seeds are pre-hulled
Your fat's shaped in balls
From beasts pre-culled

You're hooked, you're dependent
If they moved away
You'd all go cold turkey
And starve in a day

Wise up, get smart
Take a leaf from my book
Get your beak dirty
Pick your own – look:

That there's a sunflower
Go have a peek
You tweeze out the seeds
With a twist of your beak

Food grows in the wild
It's not made in dispensers
Stop being so soft
Go on foraging adventures

Get back to nature
It's where you should be
Be a bird, not an addict
Set yourselves *free!*

Tree Sparrow

Chaffinch

Blue Tit

BIRD BOX

Common name	Song Thrush
Scientific name	*Turdus philomelos*
Family	Chats & Thrushes | Turdidae
Order	Passerines | Passeriformes
Class	Birds | Aves
Phylum	Vertebrates | Chordata
Kingdom	Animals | Animalia
Length	23cm

EGGHEAD

- Putting food out for garden birds is important, especially in autumn and winter. It helps them to survive cold weather.

- When I was little, I used to thread monkey nuts onto a string and hang them out in my garden. Blue Tits would peck at them to get to the peanuts inside.

- But recently when I hung out a string of monkey nuts, the birds ignored them. They didn't seem to realise there were peanuts inside. They're too used to the shelled peanuts I provide for them in a feeder.

- I also provide sunflower hearts in a feeder. The finches, tits and sparrows love them. Even the Robin (page 96) and Blackbirds (page 50) have worked out how to get at them.

- But when I grow actual sunflowers, the birds all ignore the flower heads full of seeds. They seem to have no idea that this is where sunflower hearts actually come from.

- That's what inspired me to write this poem. I imagined what a Song Thrush would think about it.

- Song Thrushes are very resourceful garden birds. They hardly ever feed from feeders. Instead they find their own food, such as worms and berries. They even know how to smash a snail shell on a hard surface to get at the meaty snail inside.

Dipper

Aquanaut

I'm a-ducking
And a-diving
Underwater
I'm a-thriving

I'm a-bobbing
On my boulder
In the stream
It's kinda colder

There I swim
And walk and hunt
Gotta take
A punt

Looking for
A tasty dish
Tadpole, nymph
Or little fish

Yes I'm a-ducking
And a-diving
That's the way
That I'm surviving

If I kissed the stream
Goodbye
That would leave me
High and dry.

BIRD BOX

Common name	Dipper
Scientific name	*Cinclus cinclus*
Family	Dippers | Cinclidae
Order	Passerines | Passeriformes
Class	Birds | Aves
Phylum	Vertebrates | Chordata
Kingdom	Animals | Animalia
Length	18cm

EGGHEAD

- Next time you're in a hilly area near a fast-flowing shallow river or stream, see if there's a rock or boulder sticking up out of the water.

- If there is, you may be lucky enough to see a Dipper on it. That will be the bird that's bobbing up and down, up and down, then diving off into the water to hunt for food.

- Over half of all the birds in the world belong to the order Passeriformes, also called passerines. Dippers are the only passerines that can swim underwater. They can also walk – and even run – on a stream bed.

- Dippers can stay underwater for up to 30 seconds. They swim by using their wings as flippers.

- To stop water getting into their nostrils when they're underwater, Dippers have special nasal flaps.

- They also have a very big preen gland. They use the preen oil from this gland to waterproof their feathers and to insulate themselves, so they don't get chilled in cold water.

- Once you've found a Dipper, the chances are you'll see it again. That's because Dippers like to stick to just one stretch of river or stream.

Fieldfare

Far Afield

It gets cold up in Sweden
Very cold
Very cold
It gets cold up in Sweden
Very cold

So we were bold up in Sweden
Very bold
Very bold
We were bold up in Sweden
Very bold

And we flew far from Sweden
Yes we flew
Flew and flew
We flew far from Sweden
Yes we flew

To somewhere new, far from Sweden
Somewhere new
Somewhere new
To somewhere new, far from Sweden
Somewhere new

We arrived here in Britain
We arrived
We arrived
We arrived here in Britain
We arrived

Our kind can thrive here in Britain
We can thrive
We can thrive
Our kind can thrive here in Britain
We can thrive

For there are berries here in Britain
Lots of berries
Juicy berries
There are berries here in Britain
Just the thing!

So we'll make merry here in Britain
We'll make merry
Very merry
We'll make merry with the berries
Till the spring.

BIRD BOX

Common name . . . . Fieldfare
Scientific name . . . . *Turdus pilaris*
Family . . . Chats & Thrushes | Turdidae
Order . . . . . Passerines | Passeriformes
Class . . . . Birds | Aves
Phylum . . . . Vertebrates | Chordata
Kingdom . . . . Animals | Animalia
Length 24–26cm

EGGHEAD

- Fieldfares don't live here all year round. They're migrant visitors.

- But unlike Chiffchaffs (page 18), Swallows (page 24), Cuckoos (page 28), Swifts (page 54) and House Martins (page 60), Fieldfares don't migrate to Britain in the spring from countries further south.

- Instead, Fieldfares migrate here in the autumn from countries further north like Sweden, Finland and Russia. They come to Britain to escape the much colder winters in those places.

- Up to a million Fieldfares spend the winter here. They arrive in very big flocks. They particularly like eating our hawthorn berries.

- Migrating is a risky thing for birds to do. On the one hand, they hope that the place they're migrating to will provide better conditions. But on the other hand, the journey will be long and dangerous and they might not survive.

- About half of all the bird species we see in Britain are migrant visitors.

- Fieldfares aren't our only winter migrants. Some of the Blackbirds we see here in autumn and winter have flown over from Norway and the Baltic countries. And some Starlings (page 98) have come from as far away as Russia. Like the Fieldfares, these migrant Blackbirds and Starlings leave again in spring. (Other Blackbirds – page 16 – and Starlings live here all year round.)

Winter

Robin	96
Starling	98
Coot	100
Green Woodpecker	102
Kestrel	104
Bullfinch	106
Ring-necked Parakeet	108
Dunnock	110
Goldfinch	112
Siskin	114
Tawny Owl	116
Waxwing	118

Robin

Ho Ho Ho!

Do you know your Dunnock from your Pipit?
Can you name that drab bird in the tree?
Would you know a Plover if it pecked you?
No! But you sure know **ME**!

Could you tell a Whimbrel from a Curlew?
Would you know a Redpoll from a Twite?
No! But when *I* hop into view
You know I'm a Robin. Right?

Robin Redbreast
Yo! That's me!
Robin Redbreast
Yes, siree!

Robin Redbreast
Clear as can be
I've got
Brand identity!

Christmas cards
Biscuit tins
Aprons, place mats
Rubbish bins

Crackers, doilies
Carrier bags
Wrapping paper
Matching tags

Tell me:
What would Christmas be
Without the likes of
Yours truly?

Robin Redbreast
I am he!
Robin Redbreast
Yes, siree!

Robin Redbreast
Cute as can be
Season's Greetings
Love from **ME**!

BIRD BOX

Common name .... Robin
Scientific name ... *Erithacus rubecula*
Family ... Chats & Thrushes | Turdidae
Order ..... Passerines | Passeriformes
Class .... Birds | Aves
Phylum .... Vertebrates | Chordata
Kingdom .... Animals | Animalia
Length 13–14cm

EGGHEAD

● Almost everyone knows what a Robin looks like. Even people who don't know much about birds at all usually know a Robin when they see one.

● Have you noticed that at Christmas time, pictures of Robins are everywhere? They're on Christmas cards, Christmas wrapping paper, Christmas gift tags and so on and so on.

● The link between Christmas and Robins came about in the 19th century. In those days, postmen wore a red jacket. This led to them being nicknamed 'Robin Redbreasts'.

● These 'Robin Redbreast' postmen delivered lots of cards at Christmas time. And so artists started drawing Robins on Christmas cards to represent the 'Robin' postmen who delivered them.

● You know what a Robin *looks* like, but do you know what a Robin *sounds* like? Robins have a beautiful song. And whereas most of our songbirds only sing in spring and early summer, Robins sing all through the year.

● What's more, it's not just male Robins that sing. In autumn and winter, female Robins sing too.

● So if you're very lucky, on Christmas Day you might get one of the best presents of all: a Robin singing its exquisite song!

Starling

Startling

Bothered? Who's bothered?
Not me. No fear!
I get what I want
So you'd better steer clear.

If you're in my way
I'll make sure you scarper
I know what I want
I know what I'm after.

Bothered? Who's bothered?
Not me! Alright?
So what if I stab
And I jab and I fight?

I know what I want
And that's what I'll get
Ain't nothing and nobody
Stopped me yet.

Strutting my stuff
Whatever the weather
Me and my gang
Birds of a feather.

The sky threatens pink
We take to the sky

Massing, amassing
See how we fly!

The grafting is over
We let down our hair

And seamlessly
Spirograph the air …

A murmuration

BIRD BOX

Common name	Starling
Scientific name	*Sturnus vulgaris*
Family	Starlings | Sturnidae
Order	Passerines | Passeriformes
Class	Birds | Aves
Phylum	Vertebrates | Chordata
Kingdom	Animals | Animalia
Length	20–22cm

EGGHEAD

- If you watch Starlings on a patch of grass or at a feeder, you'll see that they quarrel with each other and bully other birds and steal food from them.

- Starlings strut around jabbing with their long, sharp beaks. I think they look and behave like a gang of thugs.

- And yet at around dusk on autumn and winter evenings, they take to the sky and seem to totally change personality.

- They join with other flocks of Starlings to form a huge swarm of birds that dance and swirl around the sky in perfect harmony. They create amazing fast-flowing, complex patterns in the air that remind me of the patterns I used to make with my spirograph toy when I was young.

- This is called a murmuration of Starlings.

- It's a breathtaking sight, one of the wonders of the natural world.

- And it might be happening right above where you are! So, remember to look up at the sky come home time in autumn and winter.

Coot

The Bald Truth

I'm bald as a Coot
I am, I am
Bald as a Coot
Am I

Bald as a – shoot
I *am* a Coot!
Hirsute
Has passed me by!

The lobed feet of a Coot

BIRD BOX

Common name	Coot
Scientific name	*Fulica atra*
Family	Rails | Rallidae
Order	Rails, Gallinules etc. | Gruiformes
Class	Birds | Aves
Phylum	Vertebrates | Chordata
Kingdom	Animals | Animalia
Length	36–38cm

EGGHEAD

- Do you know the expression 'Bald as a Coot'? If you look at a Coot, it's easy to understand where this expression came from.

- The white bit on a Coot's head that makes it look as if it's bald is called a shield.

- Only *adult* Coots have this white shield. Their chicks don't.

- You'll often see Coots along with ducks on a pond or lake. But Coots themselves aren't ducks. They're rails.

- Ducks have webbed feet. Coots don't. Instead they have long toes with fleshy lobes on either side. In the water, these work like paddles. Out of the water, they enable Coots to walk on soft wet ground.

- The Moorhen is another dark rail that looks quite similar to the Coot. But the Moorhen has a red shield, not a white one.

- You may well find both Coots and Moorhens on your local pond or lake. If you remember the expression 'Bald as a Coot', it will make it easy for you to identify which of these two birds is a Coot and which is a Moorhen.

Green Woodpecker

Lawn Maintenance

To clarify:
    To scarify
Your lawn you need
    No implement
No hand-held rake
    Your back to break
No mowing first
    (Your hips be cursed!)
No gizmo made
    By Black & Decker
All you need's a
    Green Woodpecker.

BIRD BOX

Common name	Green Woodpecker
Scientific name	*Picus viridis*
Family	Woodpeckers | Picidae
Order	Woodpeckers etc. | Piciformes
Class	Birds | Aves
Phylum	Vertebrates | Chordata
Kingdom	Animals | Animalia
Length	32–34cm

EGGHEAD

- Most people expect a bird called a woodpecker to make a drumming sound and to live in trees. That's exactly what the Great Spotted Woodpecker does (see page 26).

- But you're more likely to hear a Green Woodpecker making a loud, laughing sound. This is called a yaffle.

- And you're more likely to *see* a Green Woodpecker on a lawn, jabbing its beak into the ground again and again.

- It does this to look for its favourite food: ants.

- A Green Woodpecker can eat around 2,000 ants a day. It prises them out of their underground nests with its pointed beak and very long sticky tongue.

- To keep a lawn at its best, gardeners are told they should scarify it. That means they should scrape it and break up the surface. When I saw a Green Woodpecker looking for ants on my friend's lawn, it seemed to me that it was doing the scarifying job for her! And so I wrote this poem.

- You can see a video of the Green Woodpecker that inspired this poem at my website. Go to www.theBigBuzz.biz and click on the picture of this book.

Kestrel

Windhover

My skill?
Staying still
> *In mid-air*
> *Mid-air*

Staying still
At will
> *To stare*
> *And stare*

Quite still
Until
> *I tear*
> *Through the air*

Oh the thrill
Of the kill
> *Down there*
> *Way down there.*

BIRD BOX

Common name	Kestrel
Scientific name	*Falco tinnunculus*
Family	Falcons & allies | Falconidae
Order	Falcons | Falconiformes
Class	Birds | Aves
Phylum	Vertebrates | Chordata
Kingdom	Animals | Animalia
Wingspan	65–80cm

EGGHEAD

● Have you ever been on a motorway, looked out of the car window and seen a bird hovering over the verge? If so, you've most probably seen a Kestrel.

● The Kestrel is a bird of prey. Birds of prey are also known as raptors. Different raptors hunt in different ways. (See, for example, the Hen Harrier on page 46 and the Buzzard on page 56.)

● Kestrels used to be known as windhovers or hoverhawks. That's because of the way they hunt. They hover over a patch of open ground, scanning it for prey such as voles.

● When a Kestrel hovers, its tail is fanned out and pointed downwards. Sometimes it flaps its wings, sometimes it doesn't. But its head stays absolutely still.

● This means it can pinpoint very accurately where its prey is on the ground below.

● In the Americas, there's another type of bird that's very good at hovering: the hummingbird. Hummingbirds hover by flapping their wings extremely fast. The Horned Sungem hummingbird, for example, flaps its wings around 90 times per second.

● The Kestrel hovers in a different way that uses a lot less energy. It flies into the wind at exactly the same speed as the wind is blowing towards it. This keeps the Kestrel fixed in one place.

Bullfinch

Round

I'm a Bullfinch with a belly
That is bound to draw attention
I'm a Bullfinch with a belly
That is round with one intention
I'm a Bullfinch with a belly
I must fill with frequent feeds
I'm a Bullfinch with a belly
Big with berries, buds and seeds.

A female Bullfinch

BIRD BOX

Common name	Bullfinch
Scientific name	*Pyrrhula pyrrhula*
Family	Finches | Fringillidae
Order	Passerines | Passeriformes
Class	Birds | Aves
Phylum	Vertebrates | Chordata
Kingdom	Animals | Animalia
Length	16–17cm

EGGHEAD

- Bullfinches are big eaters!

- In late winter and early spring, their favourite food is buds, especially the buds on fruit trees. They can quickly strip entire trees of all their buds. This can make them very unpopular with fruit farmers.

- Bullfinch beaks have particularly sharp cutting edges. This makes them very good at snipping buds off trees.

- I once stood and watched a pair of Bullfinches strip *all* the buds off a tree in our front garden. It was very impressive!

- Bullfinches also eat at garden seed feeders.

- Have you noticed that different birds use seed feeders in different ways? In our garden, Blue Tits (page 48) and Coal Tits will flit to a feeder, take one seed and flit straight back to the hedge. Goldfinches (page 112) are scared off by the slightest sound or movement. But Bullfinches settle down at our sunflower seed feeder and munch and munch and munch. We can almost see their bellies getting bigger and rounder as they munch.

- This poem is best performed out loud as a round with other people. Each person starts the poem after the previous person has finished the second line. Enjoy!

Ring-necked Parakeet

Out of Place

I don't know how we got here
I'm not sure where we are
But I've got this funny feeling
We really should be far

    Far away, somewhere different
    Somewhere nice and hot
    What I know for certain is:
    Hot this is not

        It's foggy and frosty and snowy and wet
        Blustery, misty, grey and yet
        This is the place where we hang out
        Don't know why I'm plagued by doubt

            In a previous life, I reckon,
            I basked in glorious heat
            In this life I'm just a drizzled-on
            Ring-necked Parakeet.

BIRD BOX

Common name	Ring-necked Parakeet
Scientific name	*Psittacula krameri*
Family	Parrots | Psittacidae
Order	Parrots etc. | Psittaciformes
Class	Birds | Aves
Phylum	Vertebrates | Chordata
Kingdom	Animals | Animalia
Length	40–42cm

EGGHEAD

• Ring-necked Parakeets look very exotic, with their brilliant jade-green feathers, red beak and long, trailing tail.

• That's because they *are* exotic. They're actually parrots, natives of Africa and India.

• The only Ring-necked Parakeets there used to be in Britain were ones people kept in cages or aviaries. But around the late 1960s some of these captive birds escaped. And it turned out they were able to survive in the wild – in England at least.

• Not only have they survived, they've thrived. In 1996 it was estimated that there were about 1,500 Ring-necked Parakeets living in the wild here. By 2012 that number had risen to at least 30,000.

• So Ring-necked Parakeets now appear on the British List in category C1, which is for 'naturalised introduced species'. The British List is the official list of all the birds recorded in Britain. It's compiled by the British Ornithologists' Union.

• So far Ring-necked Parakeets have only established themselves well in a small part of south-east England. But they've been spreading to other parts of Britain too.

• Ring-necked Parakeets often feed on garden peanut feeders. Have you ever seen any in your garden? I haven't seen any in mine – yet!

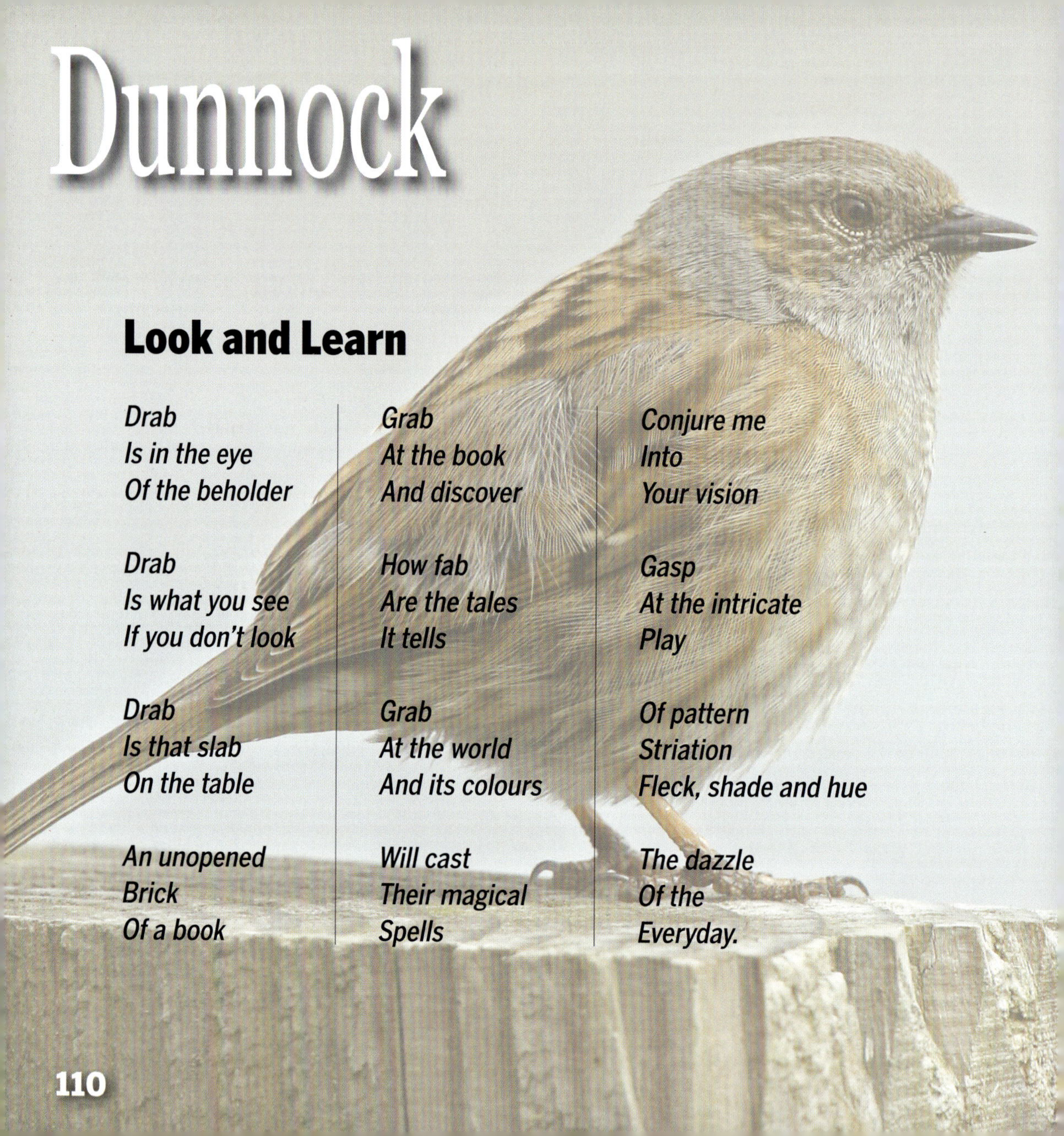

Dunnock

Look and Learn

Drab
Is in the eye
Of the beholder

Drab
Is what you see
If you don't look

Drab
Is that slab
On the table

An unopened
Brick
Of a book

Grab
At the book
And discover

How fab
Are the tales
It tells

Grab
At the world
And its colours

Will cast
Their magical
Spells

Conjure me
Into
Your vision

Gasp
At the intricate
Play

Of pattern
Striation
Fleck, shade and hue

The dazzle
Of the
Everyday.

BIRD BOX

Common name	Dunnock
Scientific name	*Prunella modularis*
Family	Accentors | Prunellidae
Order	Passerines | Passeriformes
Class	Birds | Aves
Phylum	Vertebrates | Chordata
Kingdom	Animals | Animalia
Length	13–14cm

EGGHEAD

- The name Dunnock comes from Old English and means 'small dingy brown thing'.

- The males of many species of bird are more colourful than the females. Male Greenfinches (page 20) are much greener than female Greenfinches. Male Bullfinches (page 106) have a much deeper, pinker breast than female Bullfinches. Male Mallards (page 62) are altogether more colourful than female Mallards (page 65). But both male and female Dunnocks are small, dingy and brown.

- However, if you look carefully at a Dunnock you'll see that it's far from boring. Its plumage forms subtle, delicate patterns made up of different shades of brown and areas of bluey-grey.

- These provide the Dunnock with excellent camouflage in the undergrowth, which is where it spends much of its time.

- And if you *listen* to a Dunnock, you'll hear that it has a very beautiful song. Indeed, the Dunnock's scientific name, *Prunella modularis,* means 'little brown singer'.

- It's generally only our *male* songbirds that sing. But both male *and* female Dunnocks sing.

- So it's up to you: is the Dunnock drab, or is it delightful?

Goldfinch

Collective Invective

A *charm* of Goldfinches?
A *harm*, more like!
Hissing and cussing and
Fussing like ill-mannered
Snakes! Except snakes, of course,
Haven't got wings.
OK, so like ill-mannered
Uncouth flying things.
Like witches on broomsticks
Bad-tempered and bossy!
Except witches are ugly
Not elegant, glossy
Svelte redheads with wingbars
Of flashing gold.
No, witches are warty
And haggard and old.
OK, so not like witches,
Not like snakes,
But to call them a 'charm'
Definitely breaks
The law – what's it called?
Yes, the Trades Description Act.
When Goldfinches gather
They're not charming
And that's a fact!

BIRD BOX

Common name .... Goldfinch
Scientific name ... *Carduelis carduelis*
Family .... Finches | Fringillidae
Order ..... Passerines | Passeriformes
Class .... Birds | Aves
Phylum .... Vertebrates | Chordata
Kingdom .... Animals | Animalia
Length 12cm

EGGHEAD

● A collective noun is the word we use to describe a group of a particular animal. For example, we talk of a 'pack' of wolves, a 'pod' of whales and a 'pride' of lions.

● The collective noun for Goldfinches is a 'charm'.

● I presume this is because the Goldfinch is such a beautiful bird.

● Goldfinches are so beautiful and make such a 'pretty, liquid twittering' that in previous centuries people often kept a caged Goldfinch in their house as a pet. Some people even trained them to do tricks, like pulling a small cart of water.

● But whoever it was who came up with the collective noun 'charm' never watched Goldfinches coming together on the seed feeder in our garden. There they argue and bicker and snarl and hiss at each other and are generally very far from being charming.

● You can watch a video of Goldfinches behaving like this at my website. Go to www.theBigBuzz.biz and click on the picture of this book.

● What are Goldfinches like where you are? Are they charming? Or not?

Siskin

The Jizz

A Siskin's
Akin to
A Greenfinch
  But thinner
  And yellower
  And striped

    A Siskin's
    Akin to
    A Goldfinch
      Whose red
      And tan bits
      Have been swiped

A Siskin
I see
So rarely
  I do
  A swift
  Double-take

    And discount
    All the birds
    That it isn't
      Till an ID
      I'm able
      To make.

BIRD BOX

Common name	Siskin
Scientific name	*Spinus spinus*
Family	Finches | Fringillidae
Order	Passerines | Passeriformes
Class	Birds | Aves
Phylum	Vertebrates | Chordata
Kingdom	Animals | Animalia
Length	11–12cm

EGGHEAD

- When you see a bird you know well, you're able to identify it at a glance. It has a certain jizz about it – how it looks, how it moves – that you recognise straightaway.

- But when you see an unusual bird, you have to look more closely to identify it.

- Goldfinches (page 112) and Greenfinches (page 20) are frequent visitors to our garden seed feeders, so they're easy for me to identify at a glance.

- Occasionally though, I look out and see a bird with a similar jizz to a Goldfinch or Greenfinch, but it's a bit smaller and has a slightly different plumage. It takes me a moment to work out what this bird is.

- It turns out to be a Siskin.

- Siskins are related to Goldfinches and Greenfinches, which is why they have a similar jizz about them. They're all cardueline finches, and so they share cardueline finch features, like a short, sharp bill for eating seeds.

- You're most likely to see a Siskin on your garden feeder in late winter. That's when the tree seeds that they like to eat are running out, so they need to come to gardens to find food.

Tawny Owl

Stereo

Asleep by day
We hunt by night
Eye-wide vigil
Silent flight

You know we're near
We leave a clue
To wit: Tu-whit-Tu-whit-
Tu-whoo.

BIRD BOX

Common name	Tawny Owl
Scientific name	*Strix aluco*
Family	Owls | Strigidae
Order	Owls | Strigiformes
Class	Birds | Aves
Phylum	Vertebrates | Chordata
Kingdom	Animals | Animalia
Length	38–40cm

EGGHEAD

- The Tawny Owl is a nocturnal hunter. It feeds mostly on small mammals such as mice, voles and shrews.

- But how does it find its prey in the dark? Well, to help them see at night, Tawny Owls have large eyes that include lots of light-sensitive rod cells.

- But when it comes to hunting, Tawny Owls actually use their ears more than their eyes. They have big ears, located at two different heights on their head. These allow them to build up an accurate sound picture of where their prey is.

- Tawny Owl flight, like that of most owls, is completely silent. This is thanks to the special structure of owl feathers. And it means that an owl's prey never hears the owl coming.

- The well-known 'tu-whit-tu-whoo' owl sound is only made by the Tawny Owl.

- Actually, it's made by *a pair* of Tawny Owls. The first one goes 'tu-whit' and its mate answers 'tu-whoo'.

- They do this to defend their joint territory, most often in late winter and early spring, in the run-up to the breeding season.

Waxwing

Winter Wonder

One winter were Waxwings
By Fulford Ings
> The sparrows chitter chatter
> And the Collared Dove sings

One winter were Waxwings
By Fulford Ings
> Sing Ho! for the Rowanberry tree
> Says he
> Sing Ho! for the Rowanberry tree

The Waxwings plucked berries
By Fulford Ings
> The Starlings screech
> And the Robin sings

Plump berries, in bunches
By Fulford Ings
> Sing Ho! for the Rowanberry tree
> Says he
> Sing Ho! for the Rowanberry tree

And people, they flocked
To Fulford Ings
> Oh the wonder, the splendour
> Of fine, feathered things

Strangers gathered
By Fulford Ings
> Sing Ho! for the Rowanberry tree
> Says he
> Sing Ho! for the Rowanberry tree

Then the Sparrowhawk swooped
By Fulford Ings
> And the birds, they scatter
> And the silence rings

Oh the eerie howl
As the cool killer swings
> Low by the Rowanberry tree
> Swings he
> Low by the Rowanberry tree

One winter were Waxwings
By Fulford Ings
> The Goldfinches bicker
> And the Mistle Thrush sings

One winter were Waxwings
By Fulford Ings
> And the world goes around and around
> I've found
> The world goes around and around.

BIRD BOX

Common name	Waxwing
Scientific name	*Bombycilla garrulus*
Family	Waxwings | Bombycillidae
Order	Passerines | Passeriformes
Class	Birds | Aves
Phylum	Vertebrates | Chordata
Kingdom	Animals | Animalia
Length	18cm

EGGHEAD

- One winter, when I was about eight years old, a flock of Waxwings flew into the berry tree in our front garden. They stayed for a day, stripped the tree of its berries, then disappeared. That was my first Waxwing winter.

- I watched out for Waxwings every winter after that, but I had to wait until I was a grown-up before I saw them again. They were in a berry tree by Fulford Ings, near where I live. This poem tells the story of that sighting.

- Waxwings live in the far north of Europe, in Arctic and sub-Arctic areas. They only fly over to Britain if they run out of berries there.

- A Waxwing eats up to 1,000 berries a day. That's about twice its body weight.

- Waxwings particularly like rowan, hawthorn and cotoneaster berries. So if you have these growing near you (even in your local supermarket car park), keep a lookout for these gorgeous birds next winter. And the winter after that. And the winter after that. They're worth waiting for!

- Your local birding group may be able to let you know when and where Waxwings are spotted in your area.

- See 'Over to You' (page 133) for how to find your local birding group.

up, up & away!

Finale

I squawk
  I chirrup
    I caw
      I cheep

      I hoot
        I mimic
          I honk
            I peep

I quack
  I warble
    I coo
      I screech

      I cackle
        I yaffle
          I trill
            We each

Have our own singular
Signature sound
Up in the air
Down on the ground

So open your ears
Wherever you be
This is our gift:
Live music, for free!

Bird Words

If you've never heard
Of a tricky bird word
Look it up here
And I'll make it clear!

A

aerodynamics – The science of how air moves round things.
altricial – Birds that are not very developed when they hatch and so depend totally on their parents. Altricial birds have no feathers when they hatch, and are blind and can hardly move.
Animalia – The word scientists all around the world use to mean the kingdom we call 'Animals'.
Aves – The word scientists all around the world use to mean the class of animals we call 'Birds'.
aviary – A very big cage or enclosure in which people keep birds.

B

barb – A thin thread that branches off from the centre of a feather. A feather is made up of hundreds of barbs.
barbules – Tiny hooked branches on a feather that link the barbs together. Barbules work a bit like a zip.
bill – Another word for beak.
bird of prey – A bird that hunts and eats animals.
birder – Someone who is interested in birds.
birding – Going out looking for, watching and listening to birds.
breed – To mate and produce eggs.
breeding season – The time of year when birds find a mate, build their nest, lay their eggs and bring up their young.
British List – The official list of all the species of wild bird recorded in Britain. The British List is compiled by the British Ornithologists' Union. In 2013 there were 596 birds on the British List. By the end of 2016 there were 605. I wonder how many there will be by the time you read this.
brood – This has two meanings. It can either mean a family of young birds that all hatched at about the same time. Or, when

it's a verb, to brood means to sit on eggs to incubate them.
brood patch – An area of skin on a bird's tummy that has lost its feathers. When the bird sits on its eggs, its body heat can transfer directly through the brood patch to the eggs to keep them warm.

C
camouflage – Colours and patterns that blend in with the surroundings.
cardueline finch – A sub-family of the Finch family (Fringillidae). There are three sub-families of the Finch family. Cardueline finches all eat seeds.
carrion – The dead body of an animal or animals.
caw – The sound Rooks make.
charm – The collective noun for Goldfinches.
chick – A bird that is about to hatch or has recently hatched.
chirrup – The sound some small birds make.
Chordata – The word scientists all around the world use to mean the phylum we call 'Vertebrates'.

class – Scientists divide up living things into different categories, starting with five kingdoms. Kingdoms are divided up into phyla. Phyla are divided up into smaller groups called classes. One of these is a class called 'Birds' (Aves).
clutch – The number of eggs that a bird lays (and then incubates) at one time.
collective noun – The word we use to describe a group of a particular animal. For example, a 'charm' of Goldfinches, a 'murder' of crows, a 'wisdom' of owls.
coo – The sound pigeons make.
courtship – Special behaviour to attract a mate.

D
dabble – To move the bill around in shallow water, filtering out tiny plants and animals to eat. Many species of duck do this.
dawn chorus – Lots of different birds singing early in the morning, starting at around dawn. The dawn chorus happens from about March to July. Birds that sing in it include Robins, Blackbirds, Wrens, finches, sparrows and thrushes.

display – The special way a bird behaves when it's trying to attract a mate or get rid of a rival or another bird on its territory.
DNA – The genetic code of a living thing. By analysing birds' DNA, scientists can see which bird species are related to which, and how they evolved over time.
drag – The force that slows down something that's moving through air or water.

E

egg tooth – A little horn on the top of the bill of a chick. The chick uses its egg tooth like a pick or a hammer when it's hatching out of its egg. The egg tooth disappears a few days after the chick has hatched.

F

faecal sac – A bag of poo created by a nestling. Parent birds either eat these sacs or carry them away from the nest.
family – Scientists group birds that are closely related to each other into the same family. Sometimes it's not clear-cut which family a particular bird belongs to. For example, some scientists think that Robins, Blackbirds, Song Thrushes, Mistle Thrushes and Fieldfares belong in the Turdidae (Chats and Thrushes) family. Other scientists think they should be in the Muscicapidae (Flycatchers) family.
fledge – To leave the nest and go out into the world.
fledgling – A bird that has recently left its nest and gone out into the world.
flock – A group of the same species of bird gathered together.

G

game bird – A bird that some people like to shoot as a sport. Pheasants and grouse are game birds.
gape – To open the beak very wide.
grouse moor – A place where Red Grouse are bred so that people can come and shoot them as a sport.

H

hatch – To break out of and leave the egg.
hatching muscle – A specially strong muscle

in the back of the neck of a chick. This muscle helps the chick to push its way out of its egg. The hatching muscle disappears a few days after the chick has hatched.
hatchling – A bird that has just hatched out of its egg.
honk – The sound geese make.
hoot – The sound owls make.

I
incubate – To sit on eggs to keep them warm so that they develop enough for the chicks inside to hatch.
incubation – Sitting on eggs to keep them warm so that they develop enough for the chicks inside to hatch.
incubation period – The amount of time eggs have to be incubated before they are ready to hatch.

J
jizz – The general look and behaviour of a bird that enable you to identify it.
juvenile – A young, fledged bird that isn't yet an adult. Juvenile birds often have a different plumage from adults of the same species.

K
keratin – What birds' feathers (and our hair and nails) are made of.
kingdom – Scientists have divided up all the living things on planet earth into five kingdoms. Birds are in the kingdom called 'Animals' (Animalia). The Animal kingdom is divided into 21 smaller groups called phyla. Birds are in the phylum called 'Vertebrates' (Chordata).

M
mate – This has two meanings. It can either mean one of two adult birds (a male and a female) that breed together. Or, when it's a verb, to mate means to come together to breed.
migrant visitor – A bird that comes to Britain for some of the year, and migrates back to somewhere else for the rest of the year.
migrate – To fly from one part of the world to another at a particular time of the year.
migration – Flying from one part of the world to another part of the world at a particular time of the year.
mimic – To copy.
moult – To lose old feathers and grow

strong, new feathers to replace them. Most birds moult completely each year.
murmuration – A very large number of Starlings that dance and swirl around the sky together in perfect harmony, creating amazing fast-flowing patterns in the air.

N
naturalised – A species of bird that originally comes from another country but has been here for some time, breeds here successfully and has become settled here.
nestling – A young bird that's still living in its nest.
nocturnal – Active at night.

O
offspring – The young that parent birds create. (All animals have offspring. You are your parents' offspring.)
order – There are nearly 11,000 known species of bird alive in the world today. Scientists group these species into 28 different orders. Birds in the same order are similar to each other and have evolved together. Scientists divide the birds in each order into different families. The birds in a family are closely related to each other.
ornithologist – Someone who studies birds or who is interested in birds.
ornithology – The study of birds.

P
parasite – An animal that lives in or on another animal and feeds on it.
passerine – A bird that is a member of the Passeriformes order. Scientists have so far identified over 6,500 species of passerines alive today. That means that about 60% of all the bird species now known in the world are passerines. Passerines are perching birds. They have three toes pointing forwards and one toe pointing backwards. This means they can perch well, gripping tightly onto twigs, branches and so on. All songbirds are passerines. (But not all passerines are songbirds.)
perch – To hold or grip onto something, or to rest somewhere.
phyla – More than one phylum.
phylum – Scientists divide the Animal kingdom into 21 different phyla. The animals in each phylum have a particular type of body. Birds are in the phylum called 'Vertebrates' (Chordata). This

means they have a backbone. Each phylum is divided into smaller groups called classes. Vertebrates divide into six classes. One of these classes is 'Birds' (Aves).

pipping – Making cracks and holes in the top of an egg when a chick is hatching. The chick does this with its egg tooth.

pluck – To remove feathers.

plucking post – A tree stump or fence post that a bird of prey perches on to pluck its prey before eating it.

plumage – A bird's feathers.

precocial – Birds that are quite well developed when they hatch. Precocial birds are covered in downy feathers when they hatch and can see, walk and even run straightaway. Precocial birds leave their nest within a few days of hatching.

predator – An animal that hunts and eats other animals.

preen – To clean and arrange and look after feathers.

preen gland – A gland that produces preen oil. The preen gland is on a bird's back, near where the tail joins the body.

preen oil – The oil produced by the preen gland. Birds spread preen oil on their feathers to keep them flexible and waterproof.

prey – An animal that is hunted and eaten by another animal.

Q

quack – The sound ducks make.

R

rail – A bird in the Rallidae family. Rails generally live near water and have long toes that help them to walk on damp, soft ground. Coots are rails.

raptor – Another word for bird of prey.

Red Grouse – A game bird that some people like to shoot as a sport.

ring – A light piece of metal or plastic that bird ringers put round a bird's leg. The ring has a number on it that means it can be identified if someone sees the bird again.

ringing – Putting a numbered metal or plastic ring onto a bird's leg so that it can be identified if someone sees it again.

ringtail – Another name for a female Hen Harrier.

roost – This has two meanings. It can either mean a place where birds sleep. Or, when it's a verb, to roost means to settle down and sleep.

S

scientific name – The name used by scientists and ornithologists all over the world to refer to a particular species of bird. Each species of bird has its own scientific name. This usually consists of two words and is printed *in italics*. The scientific name is also called the Latin name.

scrape – The shallow dip in the ground that birds such as Oystercatchers make to lay their eggs in, instead of building a nest.

sexual dimorphism – Differences in how the two sexes of the same species look. For example, male and female birds of the same species might each have a different plumage, or be a different size or shape. British birds that are sexually dimorphic include Bullfinches, Chaffinches, Hen Harriers, House Sparrows, Mallards and Pheasants.

shield – A featherless area of skin that some birds have from the top of their beak to their forehead. Adult Coots have a white shield. Adult Moorhens have a (smaller) red shield.

silver ghost – Another name for a male Hen Harrier.

sky dance – The spectacular display flight of a male Hen Harrier.

songbird – A bird that produces a musical song. There are over 4,000 species of songbird in the world. They are all members of a suborder of passerines (called Passeri). Birds that aren't songbirds make calls, but can't sing.

species – Birds of the same type that breed with each other. Scientists have so far identified about 11,000 different species of bird in the world.

spurs – The short, sharp bones that jut out of the back of the legs of male Pheasants. Some other game birds have them too. Birds attack each other with their spurs when they're defending their territory.

squawk – To make a loud, croaky call.

striation – A fine line of colour.
sunning – Flopping down in the sun with wings spread out and beak open. Birds such as Blackbirds often do this when it's hot.
swoop – To fly down suddenly and fast, especially as part of an attack.
syrinx – The part of the body that birds use to create sound. Humans use their larynx to produce sound. Birds use their syrinx.

T
talons – The sharp, hooked claws of birds of prey.
territorial – Protecting and defending territory.
territory – The area in which a bird nests and feeds, and that it defends against other birds.
thermal – Warm air that's rising.
tippet – The feathers round an adult Great Crested Grebe's neck that it fluffs up into a frill during courtship displays.

U
upwash – Air moving upwards in front of a bird's wings when it's flying.

V
V-formation – The shape that birds such as geese form in the air when they fly together. The birds take it in turns to fly at the front of the flock, which is the tip of the V-shape. Flying in this formation saves the birds energy, which means they can fly further.
vertebrates – Animals with a backbone. Birds are vertebrates. (We are vertebrates too.)
vortex field – Whirling air.

W
wattle – The coloured flap of skin that hangs down from the head or neck of some birds. Male Pheasants have red wattles.
windhover – Another name for the Kestrel.

Y
yaffle – The sound made by a Green Woodpecker. Some people also call the Green Woodpecker a yaffle.

Index

altricial 39, 51, 53, 122
birds of prey 47, 57, 83, 105, 117, 122
birdsong 19, 29, 43, 97, 103, 111, 118, 120
Blackbird 16, 50, 66
Blue Tit 48, 89
brood patch 35, 123
Bullfinch 106
Buzzard 56
Chaffinch 76
Chiffchaff 18
Coot 100
Cuckoo 28
Delius 29
Dipper 90
drumming 27
ducks 62–65, 101
Dunnock 110
eggs 35, 27
Feral Pigeon 74
Fieldfare 92
finches 21, 77, 81, 107, 113, 115
fledglings 49, 51, 53, 61, 124
geese 87
Goldfinch 112
Great Crested Grebe 62–65
Great Spotted Woodpecker 26
Great Tit 52
grebes 62–65
Green Woodpecker 102
Greenfinch 20
Grey Heron 72
Greylag Goose 86
hatching 37, 124
hatchlings 37, 39, 125
Hen Harrier 46
heron 72
Herring Gull 44
House Martin 60
House Sparrow 78
hunting 47, 57, 83, 105, 117
incubation 35, 37, 125
jizz 115, 125
Kestrel 104
Kingfisher 84
Linnet 80
Little Owl 82

Long-tailed Tit 70
Magpie 30
Mallard 62–65
migrant visitors 19, 25, 29, 55, 61, 93, 119, 125
Mistle Thrush 34, 38
murmuration 99, 126
nestlings 39, 126
nests 17, 31, 33, 35, 37, 39, 49
owls 83, 117
Oystercatcher 36
parrots 109
passerines 17, 19, 21, 25, 31, 33, 35, 39, 43, 49, 51, 53, 59, 61, 67, 71, 77, 79, 81, 89, 91, 93, 97, 99, 107, 111, 113, 115, 119, 126
Pheasant 22
Pied Wagtail 58
pigeons 75
plumage 21, 47, 85, 111, 115, 127
precocial 37, 39, 127
preening 79, 127
rails 101, 127
raptors 47, 57, 83, 105, 117, 127

Ring-necked Parakeet 108
ringtail 47, 127
Robin 96
Rook 32
roost 33, 59, 128
Rossini 31
silver ghost 47, 128
Siskin 114
Song Thrush 88
sparrows 79, 89
spurs 23, 128
Starling 98
sunning 67, 129
Swallow 24
Swift 54
swimming 62, 65, 91, 101
syrinx 43, 129
talons 129
Tawny Owl 116
thrushes 35, 39, 89, 93
tippet 62, 65, 129
wagtails 59
washing 77
wattle 23, 129
Waxwing 118
woodpeckers 27, 103
Wren 42
yaffle 103, 129

Over to You ...

If you like birds, there are two organisations you might be interested in. They are:
- the RSPB (Royal Society for the Protection of Birds)
- the BTO (British Trust for Ornithology).

Each of these has special membership schemes and activities for young people, as well as for grown-ups and families.

The RSPB and BTO both want to know what birds you see where you are. If we all tell them what birds we see, they'll be able to build up an accurate picture of how many birds are where (and when) in Britain.

Every year the RSPB runs its Big Garden Birdwatch. It asks people to spend one hour over a weekend in January counting all the birds they see. Anyone can take part. You don't have to be an RSPB member.

The RSPB also runs a Big Schools' Birdwatch scheme that your school might like to take part in.

If you'd like to count birds more often than just once a year, the BTO Garden BirdWatch scheme might be for you. That involves recording the birds you see in your garden each week.

And if you'd like to count birds more often than just once a week, then there's an online tool called BirdTrack that might be your cup of tea. That allows you to record birds as and when you see them.

To help you find all these – and more – I've put links to them on my website.

Just go to www.theBigBuzz.biz and click on the picture of this book.

You'll find lots of other useful bird information at my website too, including:
- how to choose a nest box
- how to choose a bird bath
- what to do if you come across a ringed bird
- how to train to ring birds yourself
- how to take part in other recording schemes, such as the Little Owl Count
- how to identify a bird you don't recognise
- how to find your local birding group
- what each of the birds in this book sounds like.

Happy birding wherever you are!

Find Out More ...

If you like what you've seen
If you want to know more
My blog and my website
Have plenty in store

There are background stories
And videos
And dates of my upcoming
Flying High! shows

There's how I can come
To your school for a day
And how to count birds
That fly your way

Yes there's audio and info
And feedback and fizz
All at
www.theBigBuzz.biz

The End

Now is the time
To say goodbye
I hope you've enjoyed
Flying High!
Remember to always
Keep an eye
Out for feathered adventurers
Up in the sky.

Other books in this series:
Feathers and Eggshells – The Bird Journal of a Young London Girl, Natalie Lawrence
Garden Photo Shoot – A Photographer's Yearbook of Garden Wildlife, John Thurlbourn
What's in your Garden? – A Book for Young Explorers, Colin Spedding
Buzzing – Discover the poetry in garden minibeasts, Anneliese Emmans Dean
Zoooo… Living Poems for Children, Hugh David Loxdale
The Worm, Dr Emma Lawrence
Slugs & Snails, Dr Emma Lawrence

If you like *Flying High!*, you'll love
buzzing!
Discover the poetry in garden minibeasts

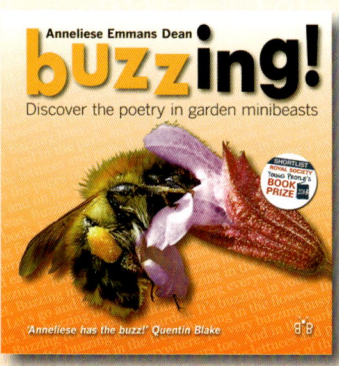

Nominated for the Carnegie Medal

Shortlisted for the Royal Society Young People's Book Prize

Winner of the North Somerset Teachers' Book Award for Poetry

A National Insect Week recommended book

'Anneliese has the buzz!' *Sir Quentin Blake*

'A fabulous fun-filled flight ... You'll be edu-entertain-amazed!' *Bumblebee Conservation Trust*

'Likely to be a favourite.' ★★★★★ *Books for Keeps*

'Very funny.' *Science*

'A rhyming romp – captivating, humorous and entertaining.' *Antenna*

'Recommended for both children and adults.' *Primary Science*

www.bramblebybooks.co.uk